"I wouldn't betray you, Gage," Jennifer said.

Gage stared at her. "Didn't you try to sneak away after I told you we couldn't go to the mission?"

"But those kids need me. I can't desert them," she whispered, realizing that by making the children her priority, she was putting Gage second.

He realized it, too. Lifting an eyebrow, he replied, "Then it looks as if we've made our choices. Come on, we have to get to the city as soon as possible. I don't have any more time to waste."

Put everything else before anything personal, Gage, she thought. *Go ahead, but that's not going to stop me from trying to heal that broken heart of yours in the time we have left.*

Books by Cheryl Wolverton

Love Inspired

A Matter of Trust #11
A Father's Love #20
This Side of Paradise #38

CHERYL WOLVERTON

Growing up in a small military town in Oklahoma where she used to make up stories with her next-door neighbor, Cheryl says she's always written, but never dreamed of having anything published. But after years of writing her own Sunday school material in the different churches where she's taught young children, and wanting to see more happy endings, she decided to give it a try, and found herself unable to stop.

Seeing so many people hurting, afraid to reach out and accept God's forgiveness, inspired her to begin writing stories about God's love and forgiveness in romances, because, she says, "We can't truly have happily ever after, if we don't have that happily-ever-after relationship with God, too."

Cheryl now lives in a small Louisiana town and has been happily married for fifteen years. She has two wonderful children who think it's cool to have a "writing mama." Cheryl would love to hear from her readers. You can write to her at P.O. Box 207, Slaughter, LA 70777.

This Side of Paradise
Cheryl Wolverton

Love Inspired®

Published by Steeple Hill Books™

STEEPLE HILL BOOKS

Steeple
Hill™

ISBN 0-373-87038-8

THIS SIDE OF PARADISE

Consider the ravens: They do not sow or reap, they have no storeroom or barn; yet God feeds them. And how much more valuable you are than the birds!
Do not be afraid, little flock, for your Father has been pleased to give you the kingdom.

—*Luke* 12:24, 32

To Bender Cove, who kept me sane these past few weeks: Kaas Baichtal, MaryLou Mendum, Don Draig, Cherri Muñoz (I love you Veraik!) and her husband, Carlos, who so generously looked at the pages I gave him of Spanish and didn't laugh—too much, and Captain (Ed) Button [aka Tarsh the Great!] who just made my day when he said, "I like *Romancing the Stone.*" You all are the greatest and such a blast to have fun with.

My on-line Christian E-mail loop, who, when I am down, very sweetly encourages me and offers up prayers. You guys don't know what it means to have support like that.

And as always to my husband, Steve, and my children, Christina and Jeremiah, who, when I finished this story said, "Oh, boy, we have our mom back." I love you!

And to my Heavenly Father, who has taught me over the past year about His unfailing love, and that no matter what we go through, He is still there for us.

Prologue

"I'll go, Pastor."

Jake Mathison stared at the tiny, perky day care assistant, unable to believe the enthusiastic statement, though he shouldn't have been surprised. Jennifer Rose was a very enthusiastic kind of woman.

"Jennifer, I can't ask that of you," he finally replied, sinking back wearily in his office chair. He really liked Jennifer, knew she was a go-getter. But this could be dangerous.

Loose tendrils of dark blond hair flew around her face as she shook her head in exasperation. "You're not asking, Pastor. I'm volunteering. Besides, I've been down to that general area several times before on the mission run to Belize."

Jake grinned at her vehement words. "Why would you want to go to Central America in the summer?"

She smiled cheekily. "Not for the heat." Standing, she began to pace. Jennifer never sat still long.

He wondered how her former boss had handled her nervous energy. Perhaps she had stifled it in order to work in such a high position as executive secretary at the nationwide business of Stevens, Incorporated.

"Seriously," she said as she turned back to him, and came to the edge of the desk. Holding up the fingers on her delicately slender right hand, she ticked off her reasons. "I've been to San Gabriel before, and it wasn't that many years ago. So, that's a plus for me."

A finger went down to show three left up. "There is also the fact that I love kids and those three kids that Dr. Richardson and her husband, Mark, want to adopt are going to need some tender loving care."

Jake nodded. "That's true. But I just don't like the idea of you going off alone. The person who usually does the run to Belize won't be back for three more weeks. Besides, Mark and

Alicia can afford to hire someone to bring those kids back.''

"But they know me," she replied, folding another finger down, her eyes flashing with eternal optimism. "I can do it. I have time built up for vacation."

She wiggled the only finger left up, her index finger. "I also speak Spanish."

Jake rolled his eyes. Jennifer was not one to give up easily if an idea hit her. That's why their day care now had a kindergarten through third grade that would be opening up next year. Jennifer had been working for the church for eighteen months now. When the day care manager offered Jennifer a job, she had snatched it up, never looking back at her past job, throwing herself one hundred percent into the new one.

At first Jake had been worried because Jennifer was only twenty-six. But she had proven indispensable, establishing herself as a hard worker with a smart head on her shoulders. That was the only reason he was now considering her outrageous proposal.

"Come on, Pastor," she said sweetly. "You know I can do this."

Jake again smiled despite his effort not to. "Have you prayed about this?"

He certainly had. Three days ago word had come from the missionaries in San Gabriel of the accident that had claimed the lives of the children's parents. The missionaries had asked him to contact the guardians—Dr. Alicia Richardson and her husband, Mark.

The couple had been devastated to learn of the parents' deaths. They had met the parents two years ago when they had been on a missions trip. Unable to have children of their own, the Richardsons immediately agreed, as honorary godparents, to adopt Maria's children.

He'd been discussing with Jennifer just who to send down there to retrieve the children, when Jennifer had spoken up.

All the playfulness left Jennifer's face at his query. "You don't know how much I've been praying, Pastor," she replied. "I'm certain this is right for me. I don't know why. Call it a prompting in my spirit if you will. But I feel like I'm standing on some sort of precipice. It's time for me to take a step. And this is the right step in my life. I honestly believe that whatever God has for me, it'll be down this path."

How could Jake argue with that? With a resigned sigh, he said, "Let me talk to the Richardsons. If they give the okay, you'll leave as soon as possible. Remember, this isn't as tame as Belize. One of the reasons we're so anxious to get those kids out of there is because of the internal struggles between the government and rebel forces.''

''We'll get to them before anything happens,'' Jennifer replied simply.

''It'd be easier if the missionaries who were down there would come home—''

''You know they feel they're needed there now more than ever. They can't leave the others when we can easily send someone there.''

Jake sighed. Seeing the excitement and simple trust that shone from her face made him feel old at thirty-five.

''Go on,'' he finally said. ''Get out of here. I need to call Mark.''

''Yes!'' She grinned, shooting her hand up in the air in victory. She whirled and danced toward the door, her eagerness as obvious as the bounce in her step as she crossed his office.

Chapter One

"This is it?"

Gage Dalton heard the shocked female voice. Wearily rubbing his eyes, he stood and stretched his tired muscles before going out to see what was happening. He had just gotten back from a flight to Mexico and was exhausted. He'd been catching a few hours of sleep on a cot in the hangar's back room before heading home to North Centerton, Louisiana, afraid to drive, fatigued as he was. He heard Sam's low tones as he talked with the woman.

"If you say it'll fly, of course I believe you. It just doesn't look like it." There was a moment, then the woman's voice again. "But I have to go. I'm sorry if your pilot can't be here until tomorrow—this is a matter of life and death!''

Something in his foggy brain clicked with that voice. Ah, yes. He remembered now. This was the passenger who was supposed to go to San Gabriel today then to Belize on the return trip with the cargo Miguel had already loaded for her.

However, the other pilot had been delayed and was unable to make it back in time for the flight. And evidently, this passenger wasn't happy with the news Sam was sharing.

As Gage got closer, he could hear Sam explaining. ''Miguel would be here if he could, Ms. Rose. This is his usual route. It was pure luck you called when you did, to get scheduled so soon. Our pilot, Miguel was more than willing to fly your relief mission since he goes to San Gabriel several times a year on various missions for other churches. You normally would have had to wait anyway since your own pilot isn't in town, so I don't see why waiting until tomorrow when our pilot returns is going to hurt.''

''Because those kids are all alone,'' the voice persisted. ''They've been told someone is coming for them and I won't disappoint them. Not only have the kids and the missionaries been given a date, but the government as well. And we know how the government is right now.''

Gage started around the corner planning to back up his partner with the very persistent woman, but when he cleared the corner and spotted her, he stopped dead. Standing toe-to-toe with the six-foot-three-inch tall Sam Johnson was one of the most beautiful women he'd ever seen. Her long, blond braided hair was partially covered with an LSU Tigers baseball cap. She wore an oversize gold-and-purple T-shirt emblazoned with the words *Geaux LSU,* along with faded blue jeans and well-worn sneakers.

She reminded Gage of a kid playing dress-up. A cliché his mom used to say years ago came to mind: tenacious as a bulldog.

Though she wasn't yelling, her chin jutted out stubbornly as she continued, ''You'll just have to find someone. God wants me there and I'm going.''

Oh, boy, he thought resigned. Another thing his mom would have loved. A small spurt of guilt shot through him at that thought. He had once been optimistic and believed in divine guidance. But that had been years ago, before his stint in the army, before his fiancée's betrayal, before his mother's lies and death.

He knew now that he made his own destiny. God was just too busy to take a personal interest in anything he had to say. Oh, he still went to church, but he hated optimistic people who hadn't yet realized that life was full of hard knocks and you'd get your own sooner or later.

He started to turn around and walk away.

Then she turned her eyes on him.

Blue, the color of the sky, connected and held him rooted to the spot. It was rare to see someone so fair in this part of Louisiana. Even he had Cajun blood, as his dark brown hair and brown eyes bore testament. Yet, here was a woman who looked as if she were of Swedish heritage.

She also looked delicate, fragile, like a rose. So, why in the world was she going to San Gabriel?

"Are you a pilot?" The sweet alto voice spoke to him.

Gage blinked. "I am."

A grin split her face, almost blinding him with the intensity. Spinning back to Sam, she said, "There, you see. He can fly me!"

"Well, ma'am..." Sam began even as the woman walked over to the plane with her bags as if everything were settled. "Gage is my partner," Sam said louder, trying to get her attention.

When she didn't look back, he hurried toward her. "He rarely flies missions. As a matter of fact, he just got back early this morning and is exhausted. He only stayed around to catch a cat-nap. He's on his way home now."

"Divine intervention," she said.

Gage rolled his eyes.

"But we can't—" Sam began again only to be interrupted by the woman.

"You signed a contract with Mark Richardson, did you not?"

"Well, yes," Sam said.

Gage knew immediately where she was going.

"It's not Mark's fault that your other pilot decided to stay over a night in Dallas," she continued doggedly.

"But there were mechanical problems," Sam tried feebly to explain.

"Again, it's not Mark Richardson's fault. I originally decided on this place because of your pilot's previous trips to San Gabriel and his knowledge of the area. And also, you're a Christian-owned company. I told Mark I thought this would be an excellent choice because of the reasons we're going to San Gabriel. However, if you still refuse to take me, all you have to do is break the contract right now and I'll go to Charleston's Airlines. They have more pilots available and I'm certain they could get me out today.''

Sam hesitated. Gage knew why. They'd just taken on another pilot three months ago. Business was good, but if word got around that their company had broken an agreement, it'd hurt business. And Gage knew the Richardsons were paying a hefty price for this trip—money Gage's company needed since they were so new.

Rumors of all type abounded about Charleston's airline. In his opinion, the airline was an accident waiting to happen. Gage also knew he wouldn't want his kid sister or even her dog flying on Charleston's. And this girl looked like someone's kid sister.

Aw, man, he thought disgruntled. "I'll fly you," he found himself suddenly saying as he stepped forward.

The woman immediately brightened. "Great. I'm Jennifer Rose." She stuck her hand out and started forward.

Jennifer. The name was too formal for her. Jenny maybe, Gage thought as he automatically extended his hand before he could think better of it.

"You can't," Sam interrupted Gage's thoughts.

Before he could argue with Sam, the woman turned incredulous eyes on Sam. "Why can't he?"

"You're tired, Gage. And you haven't been on the route in over a year." Sam ignored the passenger in this case and spoke directly to Gage.

Gage rubbed his eyes, admitting the truth of Sam's remark, but also admitting his and Sam's responsibility to their customer as owners of the flight service. "She's right when she says she has a contract, Sam."

"But what if something happens?" Sam persisted.

"I know a little Spanish."

"I'm fluent in Spanish," Jennifer added.

Sam rolled his eyes, then once again, turning his back on the passenger as he discussed the business end of details, asked Gage, "But can *you* speak it? I know you understand a few words because some of your Cajun phrases are similar to their Spanish equivalent but—"

"I'll interpret if he needs me to," Jennifer offered.

"I won't need you to," Gage muttered, refusing to let Sam continue to exclude their persistent passenger. "And if something happens we'll deal with it then."

"Nothing will happen. Are you always such a pessimist?"

Sam's eyes widened and he turned his gaze on Jennifer.

Gage scowled at her, regretting now his inclusion of her on the conversation. "What makes you say that?"

Her eyebrows went up at his growl. "Well, I can see I'm not the first one to ask you that."

She wasn't, Gage admitted. That was a sore point between him and his kid sister. "Call me a realist." Turning back to Sam, he asked, "Where's Miguel's workup on the route? I'll scan the charts and... When was the flight due to leave?"

"Twenty minutes." Jennifer eased forward until she was by his side, then continued. "You don't know how much I appreciate this...Gage? Did he call you Gage? That's a nice name. It's very important I get down there and I'm so glad you agreed to fly me."

"When you have someone over a barrel they don't have much choice, Ms.—"

"Jennifer. Everyone calls me Jennifer. Besides, Ms. Rose sounds too formal."

Sam grinned.

Gage cleared his throat, not liking the look on Sam's face. "Well, Ms. Rose, we'll leave in twenty minutes, if I can get everything completed by then." Looking to Sam, he asked, "Has the preflight check on the plane been done?"

"Miguel was working on it yesterday and already has all of Ms. Rose's supplies for the mission loaded. I fueled it up this morning."

"Thanks, Sam." He turned toward the office. Jennifer Rose followed on his heels.

Gage did his best to ignore her. Going into the office he searched and found all the information he would need for the trip.

"Just how long will this trip take?" she questioned.

He shrugged. "You'll be there in time."

"Good," she replied, smiling. "Tell me, just how many times have you been to San Gabriel?"

"Enough."

"I go to Belize on a regular basis and then on to San Gabriel from there. You do know San

Gabriel is an island somewhere near Guatemala and Belize and Honduras.''

Gage paused and shot her a disbelieving look. "You've just described about half the islands near Central America."

She shrugged. "Well, on a world scale I've narrowed it down pretty much. It's like a rain forest. Hot, humid and full of trees. The average man earns about two dollars a month if they're lucky. Their main business is exporting fruit."

"No, their main business is gun smuggling," Gage corrected, striding across the runway to the small plane.

Jennifer kept right on his heels. "The new government is trying to stop that."

"They're trying to stop it because they don't get a cut. And because the gunrunners have started a rebellion to overthrow the government."

"Are you always so negative?"

"Are you always so naive?"

She smiled. "I prefer to call it being positive."

Gage grunted. He stored the papers then came back out and gathered up her luggage. He started to store it in the back compartment, felt for his keys, made a rude sound and tossed the bags in the back of the plane instead. "I have clothes for the children in those bags," Jennifer said as if to explain why she had so many suitcases. "The family was very poor. They had one set of clothes each. Of course, that's pretty common down there. I also have the supplies our church is sending to the missionaries at Belize." She nodded to the many crates.

"Did I ask?" Gage wondered why this woman felt the need to fill every moment with chatter.

"You didn't have to, did you?" She nodded wisely as if making a point.

She was going to drive him batty before they ever got in the air. Gage slipped off his jacket, stepped back and motioned for her to get into the airplane. A small cargo plane, it had only two seats. The rest held supplies for the relief mission. A large net was strapped over the crates, holding them tightly in place.

The woman climbed in. Actually, she bounced in. An abundance of energy stored in one small package.

She strode up through the plane as if she owned it, dropping into the seat as if she couldn't wait to go.

He buttoned up the door and strolled forward. Leaning against the wall, he smiled.

She smiled back.

"Are you ready yet, Gage?"

"Well, that depends, *chérie*," he drawled.

"On what?" Those dainty little eyebrows snaked right up into her purple-and-gold cap.

"Are you planning on flying the plane or can I have my seat?"

She blushed a light pink. "Oh, dear!" she exclaimed, laughing. With a bounce, she dropped into the other seat. "How's that?"

He was still blinking at how easily she'd maneuvered herself. He slid into his own seat and buckled up. "If you'll just fasten your seat belt?"

She made a show of looking around but it was obvious the seat belt wasn't where it should be.

He sighed, reached over, pulled the belt out from behind the seat—the plane didn't normally carry passengers—and then buckled her in. A soft sweet fragrance like flowers wafted up to him, causing his clumsiness as he fumbled with the buckle. He'd not smelled anything so sweet and innocent in a long time.

Warm breath fanned his cheek and a stray strand of hair brushed his rough beard. Her soft hands helped adjust the seat belt around her middle.

He pulled back, disconcerted.

"What has you scowling so?"

The question was soft, concerned. Gage jerked his gaze to hers and saw the consideration in her eyes.

He turned his attention to starting the plane. "Nothing. I'm tired. It's a long trip. And it's bad territory we're going into."

"We'll be fine. Remember, I speak Spanish so I won't let anything happen."

Amused at her offer of protection, he turned to comment and found her with her head lowered and her eyes closed. He thought for a minute she'd actually fallen asleep, until he realized she was praying. "What's the matter? Changing your mind about flying with me?"

He hadn't meant to sound so sarcastic, but didn't understand why people prayed as if God really cared.

You once prayed, a tiny voice whispered.

"No, Gage. I feel perfectly safe with you. I was simply asking God to use this trip to fulfill His will."

That's what you get for asking, Gage thought, suddenly uncomfortable. His mom had talked that way. He remembered the letters he'd received from her the last six months of his service in the army, telling him all was fine and that God would take care of everything. She'd been lying to him the entire time. And he hadn't found out until it was too late. Betrayal. He hated betrayal. He was glad he didn't have to get close to this woman or anyone else, for that matter. He had his business, could pour his heart into that and not risk getting hurt. Yeah, that was the only way to go.

He refused to listen to the small, rusty voice that whispered there was always a way for his heart to be healed. He'd long ago blocked the voice out and didn't want its intrusion now.

"Hold tight." Gage put the plane into motion and soon it was lifting into the sky.

"It's so pretty up here," Jennifer breathed. "Look at the clouds. Cotton balls. And the trees look like those little trees you put around train sets."

"You sound like a teenager. Just how did you get your parents' permission to go to San Gabriel?" A small smile reluctantly broke through his cool facade turning up one corner of his mouth. He forgot about his fears of getting close and decided to find out a bit more about his passenger. After all, what would it hurt? He'd be rid of her in a couple of days.

"My parents are dead. I'm almost thirty," she replied.

Gage's eyes widened. "Yeah, right."

"Wanna see my license?"

"If you're thirty, *chérie,* then I'm forty."

"I didn't say I was thirty, just almost. I'm actually twenty-six."

He still found that hard to believe.

"So, how old are you?"

"What does it matter?"

"You started the questions."

He rolled his eyes. "Old enough." He had no intention of telling her he was only six years older than she was.

"You know," Gage drawled, "the heat down there is awful. They have all kinds of bugs and spiders." He didn't know why he was being so rude. Maybe he was just trying to ruin that optimistic attitude of hers.

"Oh, I don't mind the heat. Spiders don't bother me. It's just the snakes. But they're good about keeping the snakes out of the compound since there are children around."

"Snakes huh?"

She smiled. "Uh-huh. Don't like them. So,

how far until we get there?'' She looked out the front window.

He smiled despite his decision not to encourage her in any way. "Take a nap. It's gonna be a while."

"I've never slept on a plane. I doubt I could calm down enough. There are too many things to see."

He almost groaned. That was just what he'd been afraid she'd say.

Jennifer surreptitiously studied the man in the seat next to her. She'd never seen anyone as good-looking as him, except for Rand and Max Stevens. They were twins and Max had been her boss. She'd gone to work for Max after she'd had to close the day care when her mother died—the same day care she'd promised her mother she'd keep open.

Financial ruin was such an easy term bandied about in the business world. However, it was very devastating to the nineteen-year-old who'd just lost her mother. Ben, her fiancé, had insisted her mom wouldn't expect her to keep the day care open under such circumstances.

Most of the kids' parents hadn't thought she was old enough to run a day care and they'd pulled their children out. With only a few kids left, she simply hadn't been able to keep the day care open.

She'd been an emotional mess, grief-stricken over losing her mother, grief-stricken over losing the business and most of all, grief-stricken over the death of one small child because she'd broken the promise to her mother. Her fiancé deserted her at that point, but thankfully Max and Rand had hired her.

They had been wonderful to work for, until Rand had been in an accident and lost his wife and his sight. Eventually he'd regained his sight and returned to work. But during his absence, she'd continued working for Max until she was offered the day care job where she now worked. She took over as the manager for Max's ex-fiancée, Kaitland, when they reunited and she had quit to stay at home with Max.

Jennifer loved her job, but her life got very lonely sometimes. She knew the Bible said God would be everything for you, but occasionally she wished she'd find someone to marry.

Yet there was that fear, that if she found someone, it would turn out like last time. No, she wasn't certain she could ever trust someone again when he said he had her best interests at heart.

Still, surely there was a man somewhere who wasn't like her fiancé, Ben.

Part of the reason she was going to San Gabriel now was that she was restless. This was a chance to have an adventure for a few days. She was really excited about picking up the kids for the Richardsons. She knew the couple very well and they knew she needed to get out, to do something different for a change instead of sitting behind a desk all day.

And as luck would have it—good luck or bad she still wasn't sure—she was with one of the most gorgeous men she'd ever seen. Tall and broad-shouldered, he wore jeans and what she termed work boots. The peach short-sleeved shirt he had on revealed that he worked out regularly.

Father, why in the world did I get stuck with someone as good-looking as this guy, but who is such a cynic?

She knew it was bad of her to ask that. As a matter of fact, her mind was already spinning with possibilities. He was between thirty and thirty-five and appeared to be in good shape. So, she doubted it was something physical that had made him such a cynic.

So, if it was not physical, then maybe a broken marriage?

No.

Anyone who grabbed hold of him wouldn't let go. Despite his sour attitude, he had a soft heart. She knew, because if he was really a cynic and as mean as he tried to make out, he wouldn't have flown with her. Nor had he blown his top yet and yelled at her for running on at the mouth. He couldn't know it was because she was nervous. Anytime she got nervous she talked. And the handsome man beside her was definitely something to make her nervous.

"Do you have any family?"

He grunted in reply.

She took that to mean no. Hmmm...maybe there was a tragic story there?

"A sister," he muttered.

Scratch the idea of tragedy. Unless their entire family had died and he'd had to raise his sister alone. "How old is she?"

He cast her an exasperated look. "Two years younger than me."

"Did you raise her?"

"No-o-o," he drew it out. "My mom raised us. Are we done with the twenty questions?"

She grinned. She couldn't help it.

"What are you smiling at?"

"Oh, nothing." She didn't dare tell him what she was thinking. He'd only scowl some more. She'd once had a friend like that in school. The girl always scowled. Jennifer had found out Alissa was simply afraid of being hurt so she tried to strike out first, discouraging anyone from coming near her. "I think I'll try to take that nap," she replied.

Jennifer closed her eyes, thinking that was the best way to block out the sight of the cute man next to her.

But she hadn't counted on his soapy, clean scent. He'd obviously showered after his last trip. Well, that was a plus. He was a clean man. He had a soft heart. She would bet he'd been raised in church.

What was she thinking?

Her eyes snapped open.

She should be thinking about those kids in San Gabriel. She'd promised the Richardsons she'd get those kids and she wouldn't break a promise. Never again. She'd vowed that the awful day she had discovered—

With renewed determination she again closed her eyes. Slowly, slowly she relaxed and found out she could indeed sleep.

But, as was usual when she was tense, her sleep was not restful.

She tossed and turned as specters from her past nightmarishly rose up in her sleep. She knew what was coming, but as was the case each time, she was unable to stop the scene from replaying itself in her mind.

Cold white mists clung to her as she walked through the small one-room shanty. Crying could be heard, whimpers of fear, of loneliness, of isolation. Reaching out she pushed at the mist, as if it were a real thing, clawing at it, making her way through the room, peering through the thick fog. "Are you there, sweetie? Come on out. I hear you. I can't see you. It's me. Jennifer."

Urgency filled her steps as she walked around the room hunting, searching, looking for the child who was crying. "I'm right here, sweetie, where are you?"

"Ms. Rose?"

Suddenly the clouds parted. Her eyes widened. She'd found the baby. With horror she reached down—

"Ms. Rose? Jennifer!"

Pain radiated up her arm. She screamed, the sound getting caught in her throat.

"Lady!"

Jennifer opened her eyes, glancing to where Gage had her arm in a tight grip. Her hands were sweaty and she was certain her face was pale. It was dark out. "What? What is it? Are we there?"

Grimly, Gage shook his head. "I hate to tell you this, but something is the matter with the engine. We can't make it to the other side of the island, but maybe, just maybe, we can make it to the middle of the island where I know of another landing site. I've passed over it before."

"Oh, good," she said, alarmed but not willing to show it.

"Not necessarily. If it's government occupied, fine. But no telling who's down there now."

She bowed her head and said a quick prayer for God's will to be done.

Suddenly, the engine sputtered and died.

"Well, lady, I hate to tell you this, but you might just get to see some snakes after all."

"What are you talking about? What do you mean?"

Gage cast a quick glance at her. "I mean we're going down."

Chapter Two

"Lady? Jennifer? Hey, lady, Ms. Rose. Come on, Jenny. *Chérie,* talk to me."

Vaguely, Jennifer heard the voice floating to her through a fog of pain. She should know that voice. Male, concerned, sweet...sweet?

She opened her eyes.

"Wha—what happened?" She was surprised at how weak her voice sounded. Glancing around, she realized she was in a plane. Now, why in the world would she be in a plane?

Her eyes widened. She winced from the ache that action caused. But at least she could wince. And then she remembered where she was.

"We didn't make it to the runway."

Jennifer stared out what was left of the front window. Tentatively, she reached out and touched the green vegetation that was less than six inches from her face. "Are we in the trees?"

"As hard as it is to believe, we are. I need to get you out of here. Where are you hurt?"

Jennifer looked down at her body. Absently, she patted it. "I don't think anywhere except my head."

Strong warm hands pulled off her baseball cap and ran tentatively over her head, mussing her braid.

Jennifer filled with warmth. Human contact felt good after such a near miss. She leaned into him as he examined her.

"You've got a nasty lump up here, in the hairline," he said, his fingers gently probing. "I don't know how, but it doesn't look like the skin was even broken."

"A miracle," she murmured.

He snorted. "A miracle would have been to make it to the airstrip and land safely without any undesirables waiting for us."

Jennifer reluctantly pulled away from his tender touch and replied, "To you maybe. To me, the greater miracle was living through the crash in the trees and coming out alive."

"Maybe you should have prayed a little harder and we could have avoided this crash."

She shrugged indifferently. "Maybe I shouldn't have prayed for God's will but that we just land safely," she commented, a small smile playing about her lips despite the seriousness of the situation. "We're just going to have to disagree on this. Now, what were you saying about getting out of the plane?"

Consternation crossed Gage's face. Obviously, he'd completely forgotten about that.

Jennifer's smile grew. She pushed herself up and winced again in surprise. "Oh, I think I'm going to be sore."

Gage reached out, his hands hovering over her, then he pulled back, running one hand wearily through his hair. "We're not too far off the ground. We should go through the crates, take what we can use, then go on foot from here."

"No. Those crates are for relief." She rubbed her head. "Shouldn't we just wait for a rescue team?" She'd heard whenever something happened it was safer to wait by the accident where rescuers could find you.

"Lady, in this country you don't want to be near a plane that was coming in at night and crashed. If the local rebels don't get you, the government might just mistake you for one of them and shoot first.''

Stiffly, Jennifer pushed herself away from the passenger seat and followed Gage to the back of the plane. When she arrived he had already pried the lids off the four crates and tossed them to the side. He had a backpack open and was stuffing whatever he thought they might need into it.

''Please, let me go through these. I know where everything is,'' she told him.

He shot her a you've-got-to-be-kidding look and went back to rummaging.

Jennifer grabbed the other backpack she'd seen lying next to the wall. She couldn't see in it, but it wasn't heavy. There were just cloths or something in the bottom. Good, they'd need cloth for bandages if either one of them got hurt. She went to her suitcases and opened the one with the children's clothes. Taking out three outfits she folded them and placed them in the bottom of the backpack.

Gage shined the flashlight over at her. ''What are you doing?''

''Just getting some essentials,'' she murmured, not about to tell him that she was taking clothing for the kids. She knew Gage wouldn't consider those essentials. But she did. She also added her toothbrush, toothpaste, comb, brush and washcloths, as well as a few other niceties to her backpack, doing her best to keep it as light as possible. Who knew, the nearest village might be five or six miles away.

"Aw, man!"

Jennifer jumped at the harshness of Gage's voice. "What? What is it?"

She turned. Gage was digging through one of the crates near the back.

"I don't believe...this just can't...I can't believe this!"

Alarmed, Jennifer stood and went over beside him. "What? Gage?"

He pulled out something in a bag. "Looks like someone was giving some help to the rebels here, *chérie*."

Jennifer peered at what he held.

"Guns and ammo," he growled when the silence lengthened.

Turning to Jennifer, he scowled. "Well, lady, you really had me fooled with your sweet act."

He turned his back on her, astonishing Jennifer.

"When am I gonna learn not to trust a pretty face?"

"You think I did this?" she asked, outraged

not only at his accusation but at the paraphernalia found in the relief supplies. *Who'd put those things there?*

"Give me one reason why I shouldn't think that. You said you go to Belize regularly. They have a minor rebellion going on, as if you didn't know."

He shot her a look that Jennifer couldn't quite interpret. Bitter? Knowing? Disappointed?

"You also speak fluent Spanish. And you didn't want me opening these crates."

Jennifer bristled. "I go on relief missions. I love languages. And you would have scattered the contents so we couldn't retrieve them later."

"Or so someone couldn't retrieve them," he muttered.

"I don't lie," Jennifer warned, angered at his words.

"I've heard that before," he replied shortly.

Not from her, he hadn't. "Well, whoever said that to you before doesn't matter to me," she said. "Because with me, it's true. I don't lie."

"Save it." He slashed a hand through the air. Gage tossed the miscellaneous stuff back in the crate. The eerie light shining from the flashlight cast his face in stark planes and hollows.

Jennifer hesitated over moving closer.

Betrayed. That one small word whispered in her head. She knew how it felt to be betrayed. She'd felt betrayed by the mothers of the day care children who wouldn't trust her with their children. She'd been betrayed by her ex-fiancé. She could tell by his anger that Gage had been betrayed before, too.

Her anger slowly melted away. What good would it do to get in an argument when their lives were at risk? There were much more important things to worry about.

Father, please help him get over his hurt and trust me, she whispered silently within her.

Gage lifted his head and squared his shoulders. "We've got to get outta here. Grab what you can take. Whoever was expecting this plane is going to wonder why it didn't show up. Someone will report it going down. Word will filter through channels and they'll come looking."

"You're taking me with you?" She was surprised and relieved he wasn't going to leave her behind.

He looked at her strangely. "Of course I am."

"If we go to the authorities—"

"You know as well as I do we can't trust them," he interrupted. "We'd probably walk right into one of the very people who is in on this…'' he motioned at the boxes ''…this thing. No. We're getting out of here, going where we can get in touch with some of my own people who can shuttle us out of here safely.''

Jennifer stiffened, her eyes widening as his words sank in. ''Wait a minute. We have three children who are expecting us.''

''They're safe where they are. We're not. And there's no way I'm trusting you after this.''

''But I'm not behind this.''

''Then you want to tell me how these guns got in with your relief supplies?'' he asked snidely.

''I have no idea,'' she replied.

Gage shook his head. ''You almost have me believing your act. But no matter. We'll get to a city and let the American authorities handle this.''

She was certain he hadn't meant to sound so callous. She tossed her backpack down by the other backpack. ''Now listen here. I hired you to get me to those children. I'm not going back on my promise. My word means everything to me. I don't care about these guns right now. And you're not going to, either. You're going to keep the promise you made in escorting me to the missionary compound.''

Incredulously, Gage stared at her. "You're kidding, right?"

She crossed her arms, stubbornly refusing to reply.

"I'm gonna find the nearest village and get transportation back to a main city. My business is at stake here. When that mess is cleared up—" he pointed again at the guns "—if they let you off, you can see about the kids then."

She had no right to be disappointed in this man. But, oh, how Gage reminded her of Ben. His business. He was thinking of his business when kids' lives might be in danger. Disappointment curled in her stomach.

"Lahara Missions is as big as a city and very safe," Jennifer doggedly argued. "And I'm not a gunrunner!"

"Lahara is farther than going back to the closest city," he countered. "And those guns say otherwise."

"The *federales* are probably coming from the city," she added sarcastically. "If you're worried about the police, then I suggest we follow my plan and go on to Lahara. Just how much farther is it?"

He mumbled something.

"What?" she demanded.

"On this island? Maybe an extra twelve hours or so."

"Not that much longer...especially if we find someone who has transportation."

"The only ones who have transportation here are the *federales* and the rebels."

She shrugged. "We're wasting time."

As if just realizing he'd been sitting there arguing with her, he turned back and finished stuffing his essentials into the backpack before slipping it on his shoulders. Going to the wall of the plane that was still partially intact, he pulled down a flare gun, a first aid kit and a machete.

"A machete?" she asked incredulously.

"Great for cutting ropes in an emergency," he replied noncommittally.

He went to the door, which had been ripped off, and peered down. The plane creaked only slightly when he leaned out. He switched off the light and tucked it in his backpack. Then he turned to her.

Silhouetted against the starlight, his frame looked huge, almost menacing. "We'll take the rope here that held these crates together and drop it out. I want you to rappel down it. As soon as you're at the bottom, get clear of the plane. I don't know how stable this hunk of metal is or how long it'll stay as it is. I'll be right behind you."

"Aren't you afraid I'll leave you?" she asked innocently, though she knew she shouldn't have purposely provoked him. Still, the thought crossed her mind. She wasn't giving up on her mission no matter what Gage said.

She thought she heard Gage growl in response. Though a small smile played about her lips, she was certain he couldn't see it. This whole situation was beyond belief.

Moving toward the open door, she thought of how Gage assumed she was a smuggler! She didn't lie and wouldn't stand for someone not trusting her—again. *What am I going to do?* she silently lamented.

Patience, a small quiet voice whispered.

"Well?" Gage demanded.

Jennifer rubbed her hands against her legs, hoping he couldn't tell she was sweating. There was only one way to learn rappelling, she supposed, and that was just to do it.

"Here," Gage said, shoving the rope at her. "Go down this and wait for me on the ground."

When she started to take the rope, he held on, drawing her gaze to his. "You'd better be there," he warned, eyeing her distrustfully.

"Don't worry, I'll be there," she replied, regretting her earlier need to bait him.

Looking over the side she decided she'd just jump. So, with a quick breath and holding on to the rope, she ran, straight out, leaping into the darkness with nothing but the rope to hold her.

A scream pierced the night air.

And she continued to scream all the way down as her hands sought to find purchase on the rough rope.

"What in the world—?"

Gage watched in disbelief as the woman disappeared at an alarming rate of speed down the rope, screaming like a banshee the entire time she fell.

He couldn't believe she'd taken a running leap out of the airplane. A loud thunk echoed below as she obviously connected with the ground. "I don't believe this, God. The world believes You watch over children and fools. I just hope that's true because that woman definitely falls into one of those categories."

He grabbed the now slack rope and backed out of the plane. Carefully lowering himself to the ground, he saw Jennifer still lying where she'd landed. Concerned, he dropped the last few feet and knelt by her.

"Jennifer?" he said, reaching out and feeling her head once again for bumps, both alarmed and concerned with how still she lay.

A low moan sounded. Then her eyes blinked open.

Relief surged into his veins, followed by anger. "Why in the world did you jump like that?" he demanded, staring into the pain-clouded eyes that had focused on him.

"Where are you hurt?" he immediately added, as he carefully checked for broken bones.

She blinked. "I'm fine." Focusing on him again, she scowled. "And how was I supposed to jump? I've never rappelled before." She slapped at his hands, making shooing motions.

"Why didn't you tell me that!" he growled, angry that he hadn't thought to instruct her on the proper way to exit the plane and angry that she had pulled such a stupid stunt. "You should have asked!"

She pushed herself up, wincing as she did. "I didn't figure you'd be too accommodating in your foul mood."

He scowled, then saw her cringe as she flexed her fingers. "Come here," he commanded, pulling her up by her wrists.

She was so small next to him, so tiny and

delicate. There was no way she was going to survive in the jungle. She almost hadn't survived jumping out of the plane. Feeling his blood pressure go up as he remembered that, he forced his mind away from the terror he had felt and on to the obvious pain she was in. He looked around until he could find a decent clearing. Sitting her down on a log, he pulled out his flashlight and the first aid kit. Huge angry welts crossed the inside of each palm where she'd been unable to get a tight hold on the rope and had allowed it to slide through her hands. "The skin isn't broken, but you still need some salve on these."

He pulled out some containers of ointment and bandages. While he worked she didn't say a word. He knew her hands had to hurt tremendously. He'd once had rope burns on his hands. And it had hurt.

Her hands were tender, soft, not calloused like his. The large red welts nearly covered them. He should have made her wrap her hands in his shirt, anything to avoid this.

Her hands were meant for nurturing, tenderness, not gunrunning.

How could she be smuggling guns?

He was determined to find that out. His best friend, Tom, had died because he'd been involved in the black market. Gage had prayed and prayed for him over in South Korea. But Tom had been on a one-way street, refusing to turn back. He knew how dangerous his actions were.

Gage couldn't understand how anyone could get involved with that. He remembered the horror of finding his friend's body, and of the false accusations against him afterward. Of almost losing his career because of the charges that had been brought against him. All were proved to be false later, but not soon enough to tell his mom, or keep his fiancée.

He knew the rebels got the guns with the intent of throwing over the government. It was a money thing for them. Money and power.

But how could someone so innocent and sweet and proclaiming to be a Christian be into something so dirty and underworld. Unless...

"You weren't smuggling the guns?" he asked again.

"I told you I wasn't."

"Then who were you smuggling them for?"

"I wasn't."

He sighed. He should have known she wouldn't rat on a friend. So, he was in quite a dilemma. What could he do with her now?

He knew from experience not to trust people.

Tom had died all the while assuring him he wasn't doing anything wrong. His girlfriend had continued to write him even as she had made wedding preparations to someone else. And his mother...his mother had promised him everything was okay when indeed, she had been dying of cancer. He could have gotten out of the service and come home to take care of her despite the problems with his career. But she hadn't told him. And his sister had kept quiet about it at their mother's request. He just couldn't trust people to be honest with him when it came down to it.

It was better not to need anyone, to be able to do his own thing. And that was what he was doing. He planned to build up his air freight service to where it could compete with the other ones in the area. His whole life was going to be dedicated to that. And no woman, especially one who looked like an innocent but was obviously involved in something she shouldn't be, was going to ruin his chance at the goal he had set for his life.

Taking out the gauze, he wrapped her hands. "That'll take care of it," he said when she didn't comment. "Take these aspirin and we'll be on our way."

"On our way where?" She looked around the dark area curiously.

"Anywhere but right under this plane. And the farther away the better."

"But do you even know where we are?" she asked.

"If I'm not mistaken, we need to head that way." He pointed behind him back toward the plane. "It'll get us to the nearest big city."

"I told you I'm not going to the city."

Gage shook his head. He had to admire the woman's spunk. Even after being caught with illegal guns, she still insisted on having her way. "You're going to the city, with me. Even if I did trust you and thought you were telling the truth, I still wouldn't leave you out here. You'd never make it."

"I can take care of myself." Her chin jutted out stubbornly.

He smiled. "You'd be eaten alive before you made a day's travel."

"Just how many times have you been in this jungle?"

"I've never been in this jungle." Thinking about his tour in Korea, he added, "But—"

"I've heard enough," she interrupted. "I see now that you're just worried. I'm sure we'll be fine. I've studied everything there is to know about San Gabriel.''

Her words were a boast and he knew it. But he didn't call her on it. He found himself actually wanting to hear what the woman said.

''I can guarantee you there's nothing here that'll eat you, except maybe the snakes.'' She glanced around before returning her attention to him. ''Anyway, since you obviously have no idea how to handle the situation, I can protect both of us. And since that's the case, I must really insist you go to the mission instead.''

He really should set her straight on who was protecting whom, he thought, realizing his anger and wariness had faded to be replaced with amusement. Instead, he said, ''We're going the shorter route—''

A loud monkey's screech behind them brought his head around. He held up a hand, motioning her to be quiet. He strained, listening for anything out of place with the night sounds.

The chirp of crickets and frogs was loud along with the rustle of tree branches rattling overhead with the night life. No other sounds, though.

So, why was the hair on the back of his neck standing on end? *God, if you listen to personal prayers,* Gage said to himself, *then just let me get us out of this alive.*

The woman didn't seem to be the least bit worried. But Gage knew right now they were at their most vulnerable. All it would take was someone stumbling onto them this close to the plane and they would be mincemeat. Whoever found them wouldn't stop to ask questions.

Suddenly, he heard a noise—a bark of command. "Someone's coming."

Before he could stop her, Jennifer stood and started toward the sound. "Good. They can help us—"

He grabbed her ankle, tumbling her down into his arms, barely stopping her progress before the people came into the clearing. "Don't even think about it," he warned.

Jennifer stared up at him, wide-eyed. "Tell me you didn't just trip me on purpose."

She squirmed in his arms. When she was unable to move, she crossed her arms and stared mutinously. "They're coming from the way you wanted to go," she said as if talking to a two-year-old child.

Gage couldn't believe her, glaring at him as if he were the one who was in the wrong.

"That me-e-e-ans," she said drawing out the

word, "they're probably from the city and are *federales*."

Gage shook his head. "We're not taking that chance. Come on." He started to pull her up, then pushed her down as the first of the people came into view.

"Shhh," he warned, falling down next to her.

He clamped a hand over her mouth, deciding it was better to be safe than sorry. "Do not move."

She stilled.

He listened to the rapid Spanish, unable to make out more than an occasional word.

They'd seen the plane go down and were looking for something. He was certain of that much. It figured he and his passenger would still be this close when the *federales* showed up looking for guns.

One of the soldiers passed within inches of them and when Jennifer squirmed he clamped down harder.

Fusils...dinero. Guns and money. He knew those words.

Another shout went up.

"Well, we're now gunrunners according to them," he muttered quietly into his captive's ear.

Listening intently he heard a sudden commotion from the plane. "What? What is it?" he asked her.

He couldn't quite make out their rapid speech. He released his hold just enough for Jennifer to answer him.

But she didn't.

"What is it? Tell me!"

Jennifer refused to look at him.

"If you don't want me to turn you over to them right now, you'll tell me what they said," he warned, having no such intention of turning her over at all. But the look on her face worried him.

Finally, she whispered. "They've found my purse. They know one of the crew is a woman."

"And?" he asked, when she didn't finish.

"And I'm not repeating what they said. Suffice it to say, they'll enjoy finding us."

Cold chills skittered down Gage's spine. He knew then what had been said. This was a nightmare. In Korea he and his buddies had stuck together. They had depended on each other. But here, with him in this situation, was a woman. Someone who wasn't used to the harsh world of war. He would, of course, die before he let anyone hurt a woman under his care.

But would she do the same for him? He was in a deadly situation and wasn't sure he could even turn his back on the woman called Jennifer Rose.

"Come on," he murmured. "Follow me." He inched backward against the soft, mushy ground. "If you care at all for your life, you'll do exactly what I say and not give me any reason to doubt you again."

Jennifer didn't comment but inched her way back, too.

It was seconds before he realized she'd stopped moving. "Well, come on," he whispered. "What are you waiting for?"

She rolled over. But instead of looking at him, she was looking to his side.

"Going somewhere?" Though it was said in Spanish, Gage recognized the words. He rolled over and saw, standing at Jennifer's feet, one of the soldiers who'd been searching the plane.

Chapter Three

She kicked the soldier.

Hard.

With a gasp and a choking sound, the soldier grabbed himself and fell to the ground.

"Come on!" Gage said and took hold of Jennifer's arm.

Before Jennifer could grasp Gage's intentions, he had hauled her up.

Behind them rose a cry of alarm. "Jesus," Jennifer said, stumbling over some unseen obstacle, "protect us."

She lurched along behind Gage as they fought their way through the thick foliage. Soldiers shouted. A popping sound echoed loudly in her ears.

"They're shooting at us!" Jennifer cried out, putting on a burst of speed.

"Well, honey," Gage hollered over his shoulder, "that's what they tend to do to rebel sympathizers."

Under and over and around they ran, the sound of pursuit loud in their ears. Jennifer developed a stitch in her side, each step becoming agony, but she forced herself onward. She wasn't going to endanger some innocent person because of her weakness. Never again.

"We have to get out of here alive," she gasped. "I have to get to those kids."

"If I were you, lady, I'd be worrying about just getting out of here alive." He swerved around another tree.

Suddenly he jerked her to a stop. With a quick wrench, Gage pulled Jennifer against him.

Strong arms surrounded her. A thundering of his heartbeat assaulted her ears. The smell of his sweat filled her nose where it was buried against his chest.

"Shhh," he whispered low, against her ear, his breath more of a feeling than a sound.

She listened with him, but could hear nothing. "They're on both flanks," he finally warned.

Finally, she heard them.

A soft whistle, an occasional noise.

Amazed, she turned her eyes up to Gage. He was very good at picking up sounds, she realized. ''What are we going to do?'' she mouthed, low.

He shrugged. ''I've never been in quite this situation before.''

Jennifer leaned back into his body, allowing his arms to hold her close. *Please, God. Please help us out of this situation. Those kids need us.*

''We'll try this way.''

His low whisper against her ear sent shivers down her spine. Before she could assimilate the reason, he turned her around and nudged her forward.

''Hopefully, they'll think we're night life if they hear us. But no matter what, no talking.''

She nodded.

Inch by inch they worked their way forward, listening to the calls and questions from those around them. Jennifer could tell from their words that the people were slowly zeroing in on them.

When Gage stiffened she froze. She knew he had a reason for his actions.

Straining, she finally heard why. Less than fifteen feet away, the underbrush rustled. Someone was almost directly to their left.

The unknown stalker called out to another of his cohorts.

She held her breath.

An answer from their right sounded softly. The man moved forward, called out again and moved off to the left.

Jennifer's eyes widened at the man's words. She turned toward Gage and opened her mouth but Gage hurriedly covered it, a warning look in his eyes.

She hesitated. She could wait, she supposed, as long as they didn't move.

As they stood there, both men branched out away from them moving farther and farther away.

Relieved, Jennifer decided it would be okay. She relaxed against Gage in relief, thinking of how close their call really had been and what Gage's reaction would be when she told him—

Suddenly Gage nudged her forward.

"Gage," she whispered, but he ignored her and nudged her again.

"But, Gage," she implored. "Listen to me. I have to tell you—"

"Shhh," he repeated.

"Gage!" She turned and wrapped her arms around his waist.

Gage stilled. "This isn't the time," he said after a short hesitation. "Let me go." He tried to remove her arms from around him.

She gasped. "This is the time. And it's not what you think. You've got to listen to me."

"They'll hear you!" He prodded her again.

"But there's a—"

That was as far as she got. Her foot met thin air. She jerked against Gage trying to counter herself, but threw Gage off balance with her actions.

She had to give him credit. He did try to stop their fall, once he realized what was happening.

Her squeal alerted the soldiers.

A shout sounded nearby.

Thankfully, the soldiers were too late. Better to take their chances in the fall to the river below than at the end of a gun—or worse.

Down she and Gage plunged, down a slippery path through bushes and mud. Then they were airborne and falling headlong into oblivion.

Jennifer took a breath just in time. With a sudden jar, she hit the water, plunging deep into its dark depths.

She was torn loose from Gage's grasp. The

cool water surrounded her, tossing her around in every direction as she tried, wildly, to fight her way to the surface.

Left, right, up, down. Direction had no meaning. Her lungs burned and hurt as she struggled. In front of her eyes vivid colors swirled.

A lethargic peace settled about her. Her struggles lagged and she slowly stopped fighting.

She knew she was dying.

I don't want to die this way! her mind screamed. And then, her head bobbed to the surface.

She sucked in fresh air, her voice audible in its endeavor to regain the oxygen she needed.

"You're alive!"

The shout over the rushing water was loud. She turned toward the sweet sound of Gage's voice, then grunted when a hand tangled in her hair.

Still fuzzy from her near death, she struggled.

"Shhh, *chérie*. It's only me."

Feeling the rumble of his voice against her own body brought relief to her. Still fighting for breath, she didn't comment but allowed Gage to support her as they floated along the river. At the shore he dragged her out of the water after him.

"Thank you," she whispered, both to Gage and God as she fell exhausted, to the shore.

Gage collapsed next to her, his arm still draped around her waist. "I thought you'd died out there," he said when his own breathing had returned to normal.

"So did I," she said, a rusty laugh escaping.

"I guess incurable optimists aren't always optimistic," he murmured.

Another raw chuckle escaped. "Lying here on the shore I can safely say, after that close call, I'm more optimistic about life than I was a few minutes ago."

Gage groaned. "Is it possible that you could be any more optimistic?"

"Or you more pessimistic?" she returned, reveling in the simple joy of being able to joke with him after such a close call. She snuggled closer to him, enjoying the safe feel of his heavy arm lying about her waist. But it wasn't to be.

"Well, pessimistic or not, those soldiers are going to be searching the shoreline for us so I suggest we find a place to sleep tonight." He patted the backpack that was still on her back. "I'm stronger and can see fighting with one of these on, but I was certain yours had pulled you under."

Jennifer's eyes widened. No wonder she'd had such a difficult time. *Thank you, Father,* she whispered, her knees knocking anew as she realized just how close she'd come to death.

"The way the water is rushing past us right here, I'd say we're close to a fall, which would mean caves, if we're where I think we might be."

"Would it be safe to stay in there?"

"I doubt the *federales* will think we got that far. Besides, they'll have to take a lot longer searching the shore than we will going to the caves. Let's follow the shoreline and see what we find."

He stood and pulled her up. Jennifer couldn't help but groan. He immediately checked her hands.

"They're not hurting half as much as the rest of me. Don't worry. A walk is just what I need to get rid of the soreness."

She thought she saw Gage shake his head. "Well, come on, trooper," he muttered, taking her by the elbow. "Let's put some distance between us and those guys."

Jennifer smiled. "You know, Gage," she said as they began making their way along the rushing river, "do you think, just perhaps, the fall and living through it then ending up so far from the very people who were shooting at us might have happened with God's help?''

He groaned.

She chuckled. ''We could have died, if we'd hit the water just right, or we could have broken something on the way down, or we could have even drowned.''

''Which you almost did,'' he added.

''*Almost* being the optimal word,'' she teased. ''Yes, I do believe God had his angels watching over us lest we dash a foot against a rock.''

He muttered under his breath as he picked up the pace and Jennifer smiled to herself. Though she was tired and sore, more so than she could ever recall feeling, she was already happier than she could remember. She had wanted something different in her life, had volunteered for this mission to get out of the office, and she was getting exactly what she'd wished for. She should learn to be a little more specific about her prayers. But, hey, stranded in a jungle with a handsome man was at least partly a fantasy come true. Now if only they weren't being chased by the *federales* and they wouldn't run into rebels, and she could convince Gage she wasn't a rebel sympathizer. Oh, yes, and if she could get Gage to just open up and trust her a tiny little bit, then things would indeed be great.

"Here we are."

Gage trudged through the small clearing he'd spotted into what looked like a yawning black hole. Lighting one of the chemical lights he had, he quickly made a sweep of the cave. "It looks safe enough." He pulled Jennifer in behind him.

Though she had been a trooper, she was dead on her feet. She blinked, looked around, smiled at him and promptly sank to the ground and curled up in a ball.

"Whoa, there, *chérie*," he said, but it was too late. She was out.

He slipped his pack off his back and pulled out the survival blanket he'd stuffed in there. He spread it out, then turned to take care of Jennifer.

Both of her hands were tucked under her cheek and her knees were pulled up to her chest. Her hair had leaves in it and hung scraggly about her face.

Tender emotions rose in him as he studied her. How many woman did he know could go through what she'd gone through? And when he announced they had found a place of rest, instead of complaining about the cold, hard ground, she curled up on it and immediately fell asleep.

Carefully, he knelt and removed the backpack from her shoulders. She moaned then wiggled back into a comfortable position. The bandages on her hands were brown, her face was covered with scratches, but she still managed to look peaceful when she slept.

He shook his head in disbelief.

Placing her backpack by his, Gage lifted Jennifer into his arms and then settled himself onto the blanket. He jerked a second blanket out of the pack and haphazardly tossed it over them. It wasn't exactly cool tonight, the humidity kept it from that, but their clothes were wet, which made Jennifer shiver.

So, what did he think about this woman?

She snuggled against him, her head finding a safe place on his shoulder, then with a shuddering sigh, she was deadweight again. He found a comfortable position and allowed himself to relax.

She was certainly perky and sunny. She was also stubborn and persistent.

But a gunrunner?

No way.

He couldn't be that far off in his judgment.

No matter what had happened in the past, he knew that for certain. This woman had nothing to do with the rebels.

Perhaps someone had loaded the cargo for her and she hadn't checked it. She was young and trusting. Perhaps she had trusted this pastor or someone else when they told her what the crates contained.

But she hadn't wanted him in them.

He shook his head. That didn't matter. She was innocent. He could tell that from her actions. No woman was that good a liar.

Old memories haunted him and the bitter disillusionment rose up to mock him. His sister had even lied to him about his mother's health. And she was as innocent as they came.

So, he thought, his mind drifting back to Jennifer, maybe she'd known about the guns. But that didn't matter right now. All that mattered was getting out of here alive. She needed his protection and he would provide it.

He didn't need to think how he admired her stamina. After all, the trek had barely begun. Tomorrow would show her real colors. And he didn't need to admit how her personality kept him guessing, even amusing him at some of the things she said.

After all, he knew how much optimistic people bugged him after a while. It was only a matter of time before he bored her and she him.

Nor did he need to realize how right she felt in his arms. In her sleep it was as if she trusted him.

She didn't even know him. There was no way she could trust him, would trust him.

He didn't want that trust and she would quickly realize that. The only type of trust he wanted was that she wouldn't stab him in the back while he was helping her get out of the jungle safely.

Unfortunately, that was the one type of trust he wouldn't be able to accept.

Frustration boiled in him as he realized how his thoughts seemed to be going in circles. "Heavenly Father," he whispered, tightening his grip on the sleeping woman in his arms, "she is so insistent that You take an interest in our personal problems. However, I don't think so. If You did, then You would have helped me all those years ago when my fiancée left me or my mother died. But, for Jenny's sake, I'll ask You for a personal favor. I just can't trust her. I don't know how to trust anymore. I'm not even sure that I want to trust. But, I feel responsible for the wreck of the plane. And this kid," he glanced down at the body he held, "woman," he reluctantly corrected, "is in more danger than she realizes. So far only the government has found us. I don't think she realizes what will happen if more unsavory elements track us down. Please help us find our way out of here, as fast as possible. Keep us safe until I can deliver her back home. I don't like failure and I certainly don't want to fail again...through my own fault."

Then feeling awkward after that prayer, he closed his eyes, turned off the light, and did his best to get a few hours of sleep to restore him for the grueling day he was certain they would face tomorrow.

Chapter Four

"**Y**ou are such a cute little thing."

A voice came dimly to Gage through the mists of sleep that still held him in its grip. The voice cooed softly, sounding familiar, yet not.

Gage frowned.

"I just can't believe you came and crawled up in my lap like that."

Gage tried to remember where he'd heard that voice. Who in the world would be calling him *cute?* Groggily he tried to roll over. He grunted when his back met stone.

The pain jolted him and he remembered. His eyes popped open.

San Gabriel.

Jennifer.

He shot to a sitting position blinking against the light of the dawn. Jennifer sat near the entrance. Loose strands of blond hair hung about her shoulders, framing her delicate features. A smudge of dirt on her cheek actually made her look more delicate, like an urchin playing dress-up rather than an adult who had just experienced a dangerous fall and subsequent trek through the jungle. The sweet smile on her face held his attention as she cooed.

And he wasn't sitting anywhere near her like he'd thought.

"Who are you talking to?"

Jennifer glanced up. Smiling, she met his gaze. "Look what greeted me a few minutes ago."

In her lap was a lizard the size of her arm. Dumbly, he wondered how he had missed that when studying her. A green-and-red lizard sat with its head poking out over one of her folded legs. It looked odd sitting there so tame, it's head draped over Jennifer's leg like that. Jennifer was so tame, so different from the world around her, yet here she was, holding a wild animal in her lap, fitting in perfectly with the environment around her. How did she do that? "I thought you hated wildlife,'' he commented dumbly, trying to figure her out.

She chuckled. "No. I just don't like snakes. And this little thing isn't a snake."

Shaking his head he reached up and scratched at his scalp. His clothes were rumpled and his face had a good day's growth of beard on it. He needed a shave, a bath, and to get out of here—not necessarily in that order.

But first... He pulled out a knife from the scabbard on his belt.

Jennifer glanced up at him again. "What's that for?"

He pointed the end toward the lizard. "Breakfast."

Jennifer gasped. Shooting to her feet, she cradled the lizard in her arms. "You're not serious!"

Confused, he stared at her stupidly. "Do you have a better suggestion, *chérie?* We've got to eat."

Before he realized what she was up to, she turned her back on him and released the lizard into the bushes beyond the cave's entrance.

"Hey, wait a minute."

She turned back around eyeing him warily.

"You don't have to kill it. I brought peanut butter crackers."

Squinting, he stared at her in disbelief. "You brought peanut butter crackers?"

She nodded, completely serious.

"And just where are these crackers?" He wondered if she'd snapped. Of course there were no peanut butter crackers. They had nothing except the clothes on their backs...and the backpacks...which was exactly where she walked to.

Opening the one she'd been carrying she pulled out two plastic wrapped packages of crackers. With it she also brought out two small plastic drink bags filled with orange liquid.

Stunned disbelief held Gage immobile only for a moment. "Just what else did you put in that bag when you packed last night?"

He reached past her offering for the backpack.

Jennifer was having none of that. "I'm carrying it so don't you worry *what* I put in it."

He refused to be deterred. Avoiding her hands, he snatched the satchel from her. "Hey—" she began, but subsided at his look. "Suit yourself."

He scanned the top few items, scowling. "Toothbrush, toothpaste, brush, comb, *razor*." He looked at the last eyeing her oddly.

"I brought it for my legs."

He shook his head. "For your legs…"

He shook his head again. "What's this? Food? Small bottles with orange drink?"

"Originally for the children as a treat."

"Rope, pocket knife, moist towelettes…*chérie*, do you realize how heavy this will get?"

"Is it any heavier than yours?"

She lifted her chin stubbornly and he could see she was digging in her heels. He had to admit her carryall wasn't that much heavier. But he'd be hanged before he said that aloud. "What else do you have in here? What is this material—"

She did grab the waterproof pack back from him then. "Just some stuff that was originally in it as well as some clothes for the children."

"Clothes for the…"

"…children." She nodded. "And don't you go arguing with me, Gage Dalton. Those children deserve one outfit each. I left the other cloths in there in case our bandages ran out. We might need them. And I'm not taking out anything so don't even think it. I'm carrying this, not you."

Well, he could safely say he hadn't imagined her or her attitude last night. "Fine. But if it gets too heavy, I'm not transferring any of your *necessary* items into my backpack.''

She wrinkled her nose at him.

Though she'd meant it to show her displeasure, his anger instantly faded. He found the action cute. Shaking his head over his thoughts he decided to drop the argument for now and accept what she'd offered. ''I guess I'll take those crackers since you ran off our breakfast.''

At his words, she shot him a dark look, but she passed over the food just the same.

''How long have you been up?'' he asked, digging into his meal.

''Not long.''

''Are your hands feeling stiff?''

''Just a bit.''

Setting his food aside he grabbed his own backpack. ''We should have done this first thing. In this type of weather it's important to keep those hands clean. Let me see them.'' He pulled out the first aid kit and crossed the cave to her side.

Jennifer dropped her head and her cheeks turned pink. ''I know you probably think I've been impossible, but that's not my intention at all. And I want to thank you for your concern over my hands.''

Gage was touched. Listening to her speech almost made him feel just the tiniest bit guilty for how gruff he'd been with her. True, he didn't trust her, but that was no reason to keep her at arm's length. "It's nothing," he replied roughly. "We're making the best of a tough situation and we might as well not fight."

"I agree."

Surprised, Gage stared. Was it actually that easy to get her to agree to go along with him back to the city? A few kind words and she folded and allowed him his way?

Women.

"How about letting me fix those hands up?" He knelt before her.

Quickly Gage cut off the dingy brown gauze. "I'll wrap them better today now that I can see what I'm doing. We don't want any of the red exposed. No telling what we might pass that you might touch while we're hiking out of here."

She smiled though her hands trembled.

Pausing he glanced up, and that's when he saw the fear she had so cleverly disguised. Since the outset of this trip Jennifer had been an annoyingly stubborn, persistent, bulldozer of determination. She'd shown no fear, no real anger, only a need to have her own way and to smile and shrug off every disaster as if it hadn't affected her plans one bit.

But now, surely unknown to her—for Gage couldn't imagine Jennifer showing her weakness to anyone—fear glimmered just a bit in the deep blue depths of her eyes.

It made her more human, more *approachable* to him—whether he wanted it or not.

Sighing, Gage squeezed Jennifer's fingers gently. "We're going to get out of this mess. I promise you."

"Oh, I have no doubt."

But she was still scared. His respect for her inched up a notch. "Let's use one of those moist towelettes and clean these wounds, then we'll put some antiseptic on them."

Jennifer complied, allowing Gage to tend her hands. She marveled at how someone so large could be so gentle at the same time. And despite his gruff exterior, she saw just what type of man he was. He was a man that could care.

Large blunt fingers carefully washed and cleaned the rope burns on her sore hands. He was gentle, meticulous and considerate as he slowly cleaned away the dirt and grime that had accumulated from the river and the cave floor.

When he finished washing her palms, he applied an orange-colored ointment before reaching for gauze to cover them.

Each grimace or look of disgust as he labored carefully over her hands melted her heart just a bit until she was certain she had been right in the beginning. He was soft at heart.

"Who hurt you?"

His gaze jerked up from her hands to her eyes.

She watched as brusqueness quickly replaced his astonishment and wished she could take back those words. It was none of her business and she didn't like the way his gaze became so guarded once again.

"Typical of a woman. She can't accept without prying and prodding."

She chuckled, accepting the evasion for what it was and trying to correct her mistake with a lightness she didn't really feel. "And you're telling me you don't like that prodding and prying?"

Amazingly, his face relaxed and he joined in the banter. "About as much as I like a root canal, *chérie.*"

The soft gauze wound around and around her hands until it completely covered the injuries. Jennifer relaxed, enjoying the touch of his hands, the way he carefully smoothed the gauze, tied it off, then checked to make sure that he hadn't gotten it too tight.

"I've never had a root canal," she murmured.

"It's not something you want to experience."

"As bad as braces?"

A small grin touched his face. "I wouldn't know. I never had braces."

"Neither have I."

Confused, he queried, "Then why ask?"

"Conversation." She grinned.

He shook his head. Releasing her now bandaged hands he sat back.

She reached for the brush in her backpack and then for the band in her hair.

Gage's grin widened. "Looks like you have a problem."

"I just wanted to rebraid my hair before we left."

Gage popped the last of his peanut butter crackers in his mouth. He opened her packet and handed it to her. "You eat. You're gonna need the energy." Taking the brush from her bandaged hands he continued, "Let me do that."

Surprised, she lifted her eyebrows. "You know how to braid hair?"

He actually flushed. "I *do* have a younger sister who was just stubborn enough to insist her big brother help her on occasion.''

Realizing she'd embarrassed him, she smiled to lessen the impact of her statement. ''Wow! That's great. I never had anyone.''

Then Jennifer complied, turning to allow Gage access to her hair. ''What a night,'' she said, chattering nervously as she pulled out her crackers to eat. ''I had to go outside earlier for a…um…nature call…and I didn't see or hear anyone. How much time do you think we have before the *federales* catch up?''

Large warm hands touched the back of her head and then her hair fell to her shoulders, released from its confines on the back of her head.

''Who knows? I'm thinking they'll wait until it's a bit lighter out to start looking again, if they look at all. Unless someone stumbles upon us accidentally we could have all day. Of course, if they've been on our trail all night, we might have an hour or two.''

She glanced toward the opening of the cave, seeing it was growing even lighter out.

As Gage pulled the brush through her hair, Jennifer's thoughts drifted to the man who was being so kind.

She couldn't believe she would actually be at-

Cheryl Wolverton 81

tracted to this type of man. God would not send
her such a stubborn, egotistical dictator—not after Ben. But the fact was, he was attractive and
she was attracted to him. Her heart cried out,
wanting to know what Mark Richardson had
meant when he'd said Gage was having a hard
time in his relationship with God.

But asking the simple question of who had
hurt him had been rebuffed so she doubted he'd
respond well if she asked, *So, Gage, just how is
your relationship with Christ?*

No, the direct approach was out. But, being
the type of person she was, she was naturally
concerned and wanted to help.

"Mmm," she said, enjoying the feel of the
brush running through her hair.

Gage's hands paused, then he divided her hair
into sections before quickly plaiting them.

"That feels good. I hate my hair a mess."

"I would've thought you more of the nature
type. You know, brush it and let it fly."

"Actually, at one time, I was. But it gets so
darned tangled."

Over and over his hands moved through her
hair, smoothing it, pulling it closer, then continuing on. She was fascinated by the feel of having
someone else do such an intimate task as braid

her hair. Her mother had been dead many years. For so long she'd had no one—no roommates, no family—no one that she could call a close friend whom she might share a quiet moment with.

"There you go."

Jenny turned, smiling sadly as she thought how much she had missed with her mother dead.

Gage took one look at Jennifer's face and knew he was in trouble. What had she been thinking when he'd been smoothing her hair?

He knew what he'd been thinking. Her hair was like silk. She was a wonderful woman, very attractive and he was stuck out in the middle of nowhere with her. And he'd like to get to know her better.

Seeing the look in her eyes right now, he succumbed as easily as if he'd been hit over the head with a hammer. He automatically lowered his head and tasted her lips.

Without thinking, he deepened the kiss, pulling Jennifer closer to him. He'd known she was a Jenny, not a Jennifer. She proved it now, leaning into the kiss. Jenny was a real flesh and blood person, not the standoffish personality who hid behind her bubbling personality to keep everyone at arm's length.

His heart ached. How long had it been since he'd considered dating a woman let alone kissing one?

Too long.

And this gentle creature who'd reminded him so much of the innocence of...*innocence.*

He pulled back.

What in the world was he thinking? He'd just decided that Jennifer knew something about the rebels and here he was kissing her.

He needed his head examined.

"Well," Jennifer said, blinking, staring at Gage with a look of total surprise on her face.

"We better get going." That was all he could think of to say. He felt as bowled over as she looked. Never, in his thirty-two years, had he done something so stupid as to kiss a woman who was exactly what he didn't need.

Grabbing his backpack he quickly shoved the miscellaneous items back into it before striding to the mouth of the cave.

The sound of rustling behind him and then the soft footfalls of Jenny as she approached alerted Gage to every move she made.

Tension was thick between them. But he honestly didn't know how to break it. Yeah, he did.

There was certainly a reason to stay gruff and

keep some distance between them. They both felt the attraction. And it would be too easy to accept her sweet merry words as she proclaimed her innocence and that God was in control and cared and would take care of everything. Except that the Pollyannas of the world were really a fabrication, made up to hide their own ulterior motives. He made his own way.

"Did you know," Jennifer whispered, glancing around at the trees near them, "that there are over five hundred types of poisonous snakes, half of which affect humans dangerously."

So, they were back to snakes again, were they? Actually, he was relieved since it gave him an excuse to put aside his internal battles.

"Most eat birds, fish, reptiles," she continued, staring out at the lush vegetation he pointed toward as he started out of the cave. "The parents don't care for their young. Sometimes the females watch the nest. The biggest family of snakes is the colubrids. They're great swimmers and climbers."

"Why are you afraid of snakes, Jenny?"

She turned to Gage. "No one calls me Jenny."

He grunted, regretting the slip. Scowling, he

herded her toward the path where he walked. "The snakes?" he persisted.

"Why would you think I'm afraid of snakes?" She answered her own question when she glanced at a nearby vine hanging from one of the trees and stared at it as if she expected it to jump at her any moment.

"Why are you afraid of snakes?" he reiterated.

Her little chin went up, her warning signal. He should have realized not to push her. She had the bad habit of pushing back. "Why did you kiss me?"

"You liked it." He said it coolly, hoping that would put an end to it.

"Why'd you kiss me?"

Stubborn to the end he thought. "Maybe I just like to kiss a pretty girl, *chérie.*"

He wasn't going to tell her he was actually attracted to her. Nothing could ever come of it. Nothing *would* ever come of it.

Her laughter rankled, though.

"Why are you laughing?"

"I feel sorry for all those pretty girls you pass on the street if that's how you treat them."

He scowled. Oh, she was in rare form. "You

were there. It happened. Things like that happen in tense situations.''

''You kiss people you suspect of illegal crimes?'' She gave him a cheeky look. ''Yeah. Uh-huh.''

His temper turned black. She had a point. He didn't go around kissing anyone he thought might have committed a crime. Of course, he didn't hang around people who *committed* crimes. *Nor* did he go around kissing women he barely knew, either.

He was definitely leaning toward the insane side of things at the moment. She was going to push him over the edge if he had to put up with this type of conversation with her for the next few days.

''Look, *chérie*—'' he began, only to halt and hold up his hand.

Jennifer heard it, too. Her eyes widened and her face paled.

Moving his head, Gage scanned the area. ''Down,'' he commanded softly.

Shoving her, he prodded and propelled until she was under a nearby bush. He crept in behind her, making sure there was no hint that they were anywhere in the area.

Lush thick foliage molded their bodies, cushioning them. In contrast, the rotting of their bed rose and filled their sense of smell. A huge hard-shelled beetle scurried past.

But the foliage was protection. It enveloped them, allowing little light into their haven of safety.

Gage removed his pack and pulled back at one of the many vines so Jennifer could get a glimpse of the outside world.

He had little fear of discovery since this was only one of an array of identical hiding places.

But it didn't hurt to keep an eye out just the same.

The voices approached and from the loud sounds, Gage was certain the *federales* didn't think their prey was anywhere in the area. The soldiers talked loudly, calling back and forth, complaining about the heat, their breakfast, the chase.

He tried to follow the conversation as men were sent into the caves to check them out. But it was hard. They spoke quickly.

Suddenly Jennifer stiffened.

Too late Gage realized he hadn't covered her mouth.

Swiveling his head around, he saw her trying to make her way out from under the bush.

He realized immediately they were only seconds from discovery.

Without a thought, he covered her mouth with his hand and pulled her to the ground next to him.

His eyes shot a warning look as he listened intently, certain her actions had given them away. The soldiers were close, moving through the thick brush. Gage spotted a pair of boots passing within feet and held his breath.

He could feel her start to tremble with fear. He couldn't believe he'd been so relaxed that he'd actually given her a chance to shout a warning.

He wouldn't make that mistake again.

Finally, the feet passed and the footsteps faded along with the raucous laughter and unintelligible chattering. He waited, listening, making sure the searchers were long gone before he finally released his hold on Jennifer's mouth.

"I can't believe you. Do you know what they would have done if you'd actually alerted them to our presence?"

He crawled out from under the bush, pulling her with him.

Her face was pale and she was breathing hard. Glaring at him, she swiped at the dirt on her clothing. "I wasn't going to tell them where we were."

Gage, who was slipping his satchel back on his shoulders, paused. "Oh? And just what were you trying to do if not to warn them?"

Her lips firmed and he smirked. Seeing his look she sighed. "I thought one of the vines was a snake, okay? I was trying to get away from a snake."

He studied her. Her explanation had the ring of truth. Gage knew she had a thing about snakes. But to risk her life like that...

He shook his head. "Save me from crazy women who have delusions of freedom fighting."

Turning, he indicated a different direction for them to take. One that would lead them away from the patrol that had just passed them.

"You don't believe me?" She sounded outraged.

He smiled grimly. "Prove it to me and then we'll talk about it."

Mutinously, she raised her chin.

He shrugged. "In that case, *chérie*, I'll be keeping a closer watch on you as we get ourselves out of this mess."

"And I'll be keeping a closer watch on you,

Gage. Just to make sure you don't get us in any more of a mess than you already have.''

He gaped. ''And just what do you mean by that?''

She smiled with satisfaction. ''It wasn't me driving that plane.''

And then she marched off down the path. Gage couldn't help admire her guts to actually challenge him when he'd flat warned her off. ''You don't *drive* a plane,'' he shouted, then he shook his head. She was smack-dab in the middle of some dirty operation and he was admiring her.

''I think I'm in trouble,'' he whispered.

Chapter Five

"The boidae family, better known as the family of boas and pythons, live in this area. Did you know that?"

Here we go again, Gage thought, stopping to wipe the sweat off his brow. He leaned back against a tree, resting the hand that held the machete against his leg and waited.

"Some members of the boidae family are even found in the western part of the United States. But they're a smaller version of the snakes you find here. The boas are known as constrictors because they squeeze the life out of a person instead of injecting poison."

At least she hadn't gone into too much detail,

though the look on her face as she twisted it up to imitate the squeezing process did give one ideas.

"You know, I bet you could scrape the remains of a person into a manila envelope after the bigger snakes are done with them."

He'd thought too soon. The woman certainly had an imagination. If he let her go on describing, he feared the description might get worse. "For a lady who has a hang-up with snakes you sure do like to talk about them."

Jennifer glanced over at him, from where she'd been staring off into the brush. "It's important to know about the dangers an area might carry."

Gage nodded, wondering what else bothered her in the jungle, but decided to bide his time. Jennifer hadn't stopped chattering yet. Eventually, her entire story would come out.

"So, we're headed in a southwesterly direction now, aren't we?" Jennifer mused, looking across a small field they'd come to.

Absently, Gage nodded. "That's right."

"Do you think those soldiers were looking for us?"

Pulling his gaze from the small field he'd spotted through the trees, he focused on her.

"They're probably the same police force that chased us last night. So, yes, I imagine they're still looking for us. It is possible though, they're hunting rebels."

Though he shrugged nonchalantly, he studied her carefully, watching for a reaction. He just couldn't figure her out. She acted so innocent of everything. But the fact remained, the guns had been in the crates they carried and she'd been nervous when he had opened them.

"You realize of course, we're headed in the direction of Lahara Missions."

Gage took that as his cue to start walking again. "Only temporarily."

Jennifer immediately caught up with him. "You're being unreasonably stubborn, Gage."

He shrugged, pushing gently at the overgrowth of vegetation, doing his best to leave no trail. "When you tell me why you're really here, then we might talk about the mission. Until then, I have to get to the nearest city and call my office."

"Why do you refuse to believe I came after those kids?"

Gage glanced over at Jennifer who was keeping pace with him, huffing and puffing as she also pushed leaves out of the way. "I don't disbelieve you about that. However, I don't believe those kids are as important as you claim. Everyone has an agenda. Those guns show exactly what type of person you are. Your agenda comes first. No matter what.''

She crossed her eyes at him. "I did *not* smuggle those guns. Do you have a hearing problem, Gage? Haven't you ever trusted anybody's word?''

He stopped again, only for a moment, a scowl spreading across his face. "Too many times. But never again.''

With renewed force he pushed through the vegetation and cautiously skirted the field.

Jennifer stayed right behind him, surprised and enlightened by his words. She'd been trudging along for what seemed like hours, doing her best not to jump at every vine that occasionally fell her way, trying to figure out just why Gage wouldn't take her to the mission.

And now she had a glimmer of light into the darkness. Trust. He did not trust anyone. *Please, Father, help me to understand this situation and not lose my temper.*

"Why is it so important to call your business?'' she asked more softly. "Why can't we just go to the mission and call from there?''

Gage continued his trek along the edge of the jungle, avoiding the open area of the field. Jennifer didn't question his actions, deciding he knew what was best even if he wasn't going to answer her other question. He surprised her when he finally said, "My business comes first. I've learned that a business doesn't disappoint you, *chérie,* only people. And whoever got you into the mess you're in is only going to end up disappointing you, if you want an unsolicited opinion."

"That's fine. I'm not scared of opinions."

"Meaning I am?"

The effrontery in his voice amused her. She dared not say so, though. "So, you would rather pour all of your energy and emotion into your business than into relationships?"

"You don't give up, do you?"

She grinned though he couldn't see it. "Not me. I keep going and going and—"

"I get the idea. You're like a dog with a bone."

"I prefer my description better."

He sighed. "Fine. No. I don't care for relationships. I will never get involved again. They're useless, a pack of lies built on someone's needs or wants without any commitment behind them.''

Whatever she had been expecting, that grim description had not been it. ''I see.''

So much for the wild attraction she felt and thought he returned for her. *It's for the best, Father. I was crazy to even entertain such an idea since he is going through so much anyway.*

''Do you?'' he asked as if now that the dam was open he was unable to stop. ''Have you ever been lied to, *chérie?* Over and over again. By your best friend, your fiancée, your mom? Try trusting over and over and finding out each time that the others didn't really mean what they said. 'I'm telling you the truth,''' he mimicked, then laughed. '''I need commitment. I'll be praying for you while you're gone. I'll protect you.''' Taking a breath he continued, only this time his voice took on a husky, choked quality. '''I'm okay, dear. Mom's okay, Big Brother...''' he trailed off.

Jennifer didn't think he even remembered she was there. He kept walking, his stride eating up the ground until she was almost jogging to keep up with him.

Her heart broke. She knew a bit of what he was going through, though a parent had never betrayed her. "Have you ever gone to God and asked Him to help you?"

Her breathless voice caught his attention and he immediately slowed. But though he took in her physical account, he didn't appreciate her question. "I don't believe God takes a personal interest in the individual person. I've learned that the hard way. I still read my Bible, pray, go to church, but I'm not spending my time asking for personal favors."

Jennifer's eyes widened in dismay. "You're looking at God wrong, Gage. True, He's omnipotent and Ruler of all, but you're forgetting He's also a father and wants us to come to Him when we're in pain. He wants us to come like children, with simple faith—"

"Save it. I've heard it all from my sister."

"Well, at least you have a levelheaded sister."

They arrived on the other side of the field. Gage paused to turn to her. "Don't you ever shut up? Or even take a hint?"

Jennifer smiled. "Not a chance. Why?"

He shook his head. "Because you're driving me crazy."

She took that as a good sign. Smiling, she strolled up and patted him on the arm. "Good."

Then she stepped past him and reentered the forest, thinking he hadn't heard the last of this. Nor was she about to give up on those children just because he had a few problems.

Chapter Six

"Look what I found."

Gage stopped by a tree and picked some papayas.

"Lunchtime," Jennifer said enthusiastically, greedily accepting the fruit Gage offered. She wiped it on her shirt, then took a bite out of it. Closing her eyes, she sighed. "This is much *much* better than peanut butter crackers and orange drink."

Gage watched her, amused, as she munched ravenously on the fruit, devouring every bit of it.

His mouth twisted in a grin, he handed her another one when she was done. She was beautiful, the way her eyes closed, her lashes falling softly against her cheeks, as she scrunched her nose up and made muffled noises to indicate her pleasure. Gage didn't think he'd ever seen anyone eat quite the way Jenny did.

"Were you hungry, *chérie?*"

She opened her eyes, studying him as if she thought he might be teasing her. "It's been at least five hours since we ate. What is it, eleven, twelve? I usually eat every couple of hours." She shrugged, taking another bite. "I always have. And besides, I love fruit."

Her eyes drifted closed and she grinned again, wrinkling her nose before sinking her teeth into the thick juicy fruit. "You know," she said between bites, "I've heard the people of this area will dry this fruit out and soak it in sugar to make a wonderful treat."

"That's right. I've had it before." Gage finally took a bite of his own fruit, thinking Jennifer was correct, this was good. His stomach rumbled in agreement. "I don't get down this way much, but the people here have some really good basic food."

"I'm surprised to hear you say that, being Cajun and all."

He chuckled, took another savoring bite before quickly finishing it off, then grabbed another piece of fruit. "What, *chérie,* do you only think I eat smothered chicken, or *étouffée,* or perhaps *sauce piquante* or *court bouillion.*"

Her eyes widened. "Well, I've heard of the first ones, but what's *coo-be-yaunt?*"

He chuckled at the way she pronounced the word so carefully. "Like spaghetti with fish and a red sauce. Except that you put it over rice." He frowned. "Well, there are some who put it over noodles. It's better with rice, though. However, the point is," he said as he finished off his second piece of fruit, "I like to try simple meals with different spices."

She shook her head. "I wouldn't have thought you were so versatile."

"Why's that?" he asked, surprised.

"Because you won't even try to trust me."

Gage tossed the last piece of fruit and stood. "It'll be raining soon. That's one thing you can count on here. I suggest we set up a small shelter and take an afternoon rest. Then we can go ahead and travel when the rain lets up."

"That sounds good."

He hated the way she suddenly withdrew. But

maybe that was good since she'd distracted him like crazy all morning, asking annoying questions. The questions made him remember that the attraction he felt for her could go nowhere.

Tromping over into a bigger clearing away from the path, he pulled out the two ponchos he'd packed and some rope. He neatly strung the rope between two trees, tied the ponchos together, then anchored them. It was easy to pull the rest tight after that and within minutes, he had a serviceable shelter erected.

Jerking out his survival blanket, he tossed it on the ground then motioned for Jennifer to crawl under.

"It's still awfully humid to be lying on this, isn't it?"

"It won't be for long."

She sighed, nodded, then scooted under. Taking her backpack off, she dropped it near the top of the blanket as a pillow before lying down.

When she was situated, Gage snatched up his backpack and started under the shelter.

Jennifer jumped, her eyes widening.

"You didn't think I was going to sit out there in the rain did you?"

"I hadn't really thought about it," she replied, relaxing as she made extra room for Gage.

"Good." But it wasn't good. Moving around, trying to get comfortable brought him too close to Jenny. He could see tiny laugh lines that were starting to form near her eyes, note each color in the loose strands of hair that had escaped the French braid he'd put her hair in that morning.

Despite his best intentions, he was drawn to her.

And he didn't want a woman who was going to tell him over and over that God took a personal interest in his life. He didn't want to deal with that, didn't want to think about that. He was mad and was going to stay mad. Anger was the only thing that had got him through the pain and grief all those years ago. He wasn't changing now.

Why was it people always thought they knew what was best for his life? Both his physical and his spiritual well-being.

He turned his mind away from the debate that had been going over and over in his mind lately, and onto the forest around them. "Do you hear the birds?"

Jennifer chuckled and the sound affected Gage more than he cared to admit.

"How could I not?"

The woman looked beautiful, sounded beautiful and had a beautiful personality—*just a bit too nosy,* he thought to add. *And the guns. Remember the guns.*

"They have over 623 cataloged birds here, from what I've heard," Gage commented, trying to get his mind off the woman next to him.

"I didn't know you knew that much about San Gabriel." She sounded impressed.

It figured.

"I fly planes for a living. I make delivery stops and people talk."

"I guess there wouldn't be much else to do but talk, huh?"

He shook his head, thinking of the many people he'd met who felt it their duty to share every detail of their hometown with him. "Nope. I also know that on this island, though the primary language is Spanish, a few of the people also speak a Creole-type English and the Mayan language."

"But those two are very small percentages of the people."

"True. People from Belize or one of the other areas probably migrated over, bringing their language with them."

"So, you like history?"

Gage smiled, relaxing, stacking his hands behind his head. "I find languages fascinating. I've never had much time to learn them, though. I've always been too busy doing other things."

"Oh, Gage," Jennifer said and she sounded truly distressed. He looked over and met her gaze.

"What?"

"You should take time for that. I bet you're one of those people who has always worried about pleasing everyone else and never taken any time..."

At his scowl, she stopped and shrugged. "It takes one to know one."

He itched to ask her, but knew if he did, it would open the door to more questions. Yet, he couldn't help himself. "What do you mean?"

He could kick himself. *Just keep your mouth shut, Gage. You're gonna get yourself in trouble.*

"I was once like that. I still am, to a point, though I still do tend to try to fix things occasionally."

He remembered her promise to take care of him and thought, at least on this, she was telling the truth.

"I have learned over the years that you should find one thing you truly enjoy and work at that. It can be a real blessing," she said smiling.

"And what is it *you* have found that's so interesting that it's kept you occupied for years?" he asked gruffly.

His heart went crazy when she sent him that sideways smile, teasingly grinning at him as she squinted her eyes as though she was about to reveal some big secret.

She smiled and he automatically responded with an encouraging grin.

"Languages."

"Languages? As in plural?"

She nodded and he'd swear she blushed. "Yes, several."

Cocking his head he rolled slightly toward her, studying her. "Okay. I know you speak *and understand* Spanish. What other language do you speak or understand?"

"French as well as Cajun French."

"Oh, *sans doute,*" he said, disbelief rife in

his voice. "You can say that because you know it's my language."

"No, there's no doubt," she replied, smiling. "I do speak your language."

"And French?"

"They're not *that* different."

"Well, that's nice. Two and a half languages. I'll give you that."

She smiled sheepishly. "Did I say they were the only ones?"

Intrigued, he turned more fully toward her. "What other languages do you speak?"

"I also speak Italian, Portuguese, German and American Sign Language."

He shook his head in stunned disbelief. He could ask her to speak a few words to prove it, but he wouldn't know if she was telling the truth or not. "Did you major in languages?"

Her laughter again filled the air. "I never finished college. Actually, I have a good ear. I picked up some Cajun French around town when I was very young, so a friend of my mother's began tutoring me. It was good, since some of the children at the day care center..." Her smile faltered slightly. "But when I went to work for Stevens, Incorporated I had to learn a couple of the other languages since we dealt with those countries. My easy grasp of languages is actually what got me the job.''

''But you said you had to learn.'' Gage furrowed his brow, confused.

She smiled. ''When I walked in to interview with Rand Stevens, he said something in Cajun over the phone to his brother. When he hung up, I immediately introduced myself in his language. After talking, when he found out that I hadn't been raised speaking French, he was most impressed. He said I spoke it like a native, then he asked me if I could learn a few other languages. And so, I went through crash courses in Italian and French. The German I worked on until I found a correspondence course to take. And then the American Sign Language, I taught myself, but learned exact usage when someone came to our church and taught a class.

Gage nodded, impressed. ''I'll have to be careful what I say around you.''

Jennifer made a moue of disappointment. ''I knew there was a reason I shouldn't tell you that.''

Suspicion flared in his mind and must have shown on his face because the teasing disap-

peared. "Well, I think I'll just get some rest."
Jennifer closed her eyes.

Disappointed, Gage lay back. He frowned,
wishing he wasn't feeling so torn. Could he or
could he not trust the woman next to him? Did
he even want to?

No.

Because he knew how that would end up. In
the end, she'd betray him for her own well-
being. What she wanted would come before anything that might develop between them.

With a sigh, Gage closed his eyes vowing to
keep an ear tuned to Jennifer until he could figure out just how she was involved in the mess.

"Please, God, protect me from snakes...please,
God, protect me from snakes...please, God, protect me from snakes...."

Why, oh why had she acted so impulsively
and left Gage lying there under the ponchos
sound asleep?

Grimly Jennifer wiped the sweat and leftover
rain from her face.

"Idiot. That's what you are. You're an idiot.
Please, God, send the snakes the other way...."

Pushing at her scraggly hair, she continued

on, forcing her way through the vegetation along the small path that led in the direction of Lahara Missions. "But I just had to get to those kids, Father. I couldn't wait. There's no way Gage was going to change his mind. I tried to be patient. But patience isn't one of my qualities. Besides, I just don't trust him. He's too dictatorial."

A small voice touched her heart with softly spoken words. *He's been hurt.*

She did her best to ignore the voice and hang on to her indignation. But the slapping of the branches and the slick ground wouldn't let her.

"This was so much easier when Gage was here." She hadn't realized how he'd held the branches back to help her passage or how he'd made sure she didn't slip and slide on the cushion of vegetation beneath her feet.

A verse came to her. "Those that wait upon the Lord shall renew their strength."

"Wait on God? Wait on *Gage?* Why?"

A slimy palm branch chose that minute to slap her across the face and she staggered. "Ugh. Those kids are depending on me. So are the missionaries. I can't trust someone like that. He wouldn't bend. He has no desire to help, doesn't care one whit about those kids. There's no way, no matter what, he'd go after them. He's too busy making a success of his business to worry about three little kids.'' Bitterness tinged her voice and she was embarrassed. Evidently her pain over her ex-fiancé affected her more than she realized.

''Well, I'm not waiting. That's just how it is. I am not going to stay with him and end up being dragged in the opposite direction back to some city where Gage thinks the 'little woman' has to go.''

A sudden racket above her head made her pause. She listened intently, wondering what had stirred up everything.

She wondered if a snake slithering through the trees might cause that...

''*N'importe!* Never mind, I'll make sure—''

Wait on him? Gage was already here. Oh, dear. She didn't want to go back with him in defeat. How humiliating to be found here, standing, staring at nothing, looking lost. Perhaps she'd just hide.

With that in mind, she pushed back into the vegetation, thinking he would pass her right by and never know she was there if she could get back far enough. Just a bit more and he wouldn't see her.

Just a bit more...

"Aaarrgh!"

Her foot met the ground and sank. She wind-milled, trying to keep her balance, teetering back and forth.

With a sense of I-knew-it-was-going-to-happen-anyway, she fell backward.

Jennifer closed her eyes, envisioning another slide down a hill and into a river below.

Instead, her rear met with a soft, squishy splat.

Chapter Seven

"Oh, ugh!" Cool, thick sludge covered her from the waist up. She lifted her hands and watched as brown muck fell off in great big blops.

"Well, *chérie*, I see you decided to take a mud bath while I rested."

Glowering, Jennifer raised her gaze to Gage's. Though he smiled, his gaze plainly said he was mad.

She just hated getting caught.

Wait upon the Lord and you shall renew your strength.

Ignore warnings from God and look what it gets you.

She tried to look innocent even though she knew he'd meant the comment as sarcastic. They both knew why she was where she was. But she didn't have to argue with him about it. "It's quite nice. Took me a while to find enough mud, though."

"I'll just bet it did. Exactly," he paused and looked at his watch, "two hours and forty-five minutes."

She widened her eyes. "That long?"

He nodded.

"Well, you would think in a jungle this size, you could find a mud hole faster than that."

He crossed his arms. "Are you going to get out of there now? We have lost time to make up for."

He wasn't going to offer to help her and she wasn't going to ask for help. She could tell by his smug smile he was now waiting for her to ask. Glancing around, she saw a big palm leaf sticking out from one of the plants. With a smile at Gage, she reached out and grabbed it and tried to haul herself out of the mud.

A loud sucking noise mixed with the sloshing and then with a snap as the leaf broke. Jennifer went flying backward. With a screech, she fell, the mire covering her head this time.

Frantically her arms shot up out of the mud in mute appeal.

Warm strong hands immediately circled her wrists. With a steady, firm grip she was lifted from the gunk.

"Oh, double ugh—" she stopped and spit because the sludge oozed into her mouth when she opened it to complain.

"Just be still a second and let me help wipe that off your face before you swallow it."

She stood in the muck almost to her knees and didn't comment. Instead, Jennifer continued to try to push the nasty tasting floor decay out of her mouth with her tongue as Gage methodically wiped it off her face.

"You owe me a pair of boots for this," he muttered, wiping at her ears and then her neck, trailing the cloth over her skin.

Jennifer stilled.

There was that personal touch again, something she had so rarely experienced.

It felt so nice. And Gage was really a nice guy despite how much he could drive her crazy with his demands that she return to some town in the opposite direction.

Jennifer's eyes drifted open, her gaze lifting to Gage's. He was focused on her neck where he wiped, wearing a determined mask as he worked to get the mud off.

As if sensing her scrutiny he glanced up from her neck to her eyes. Their gazes locked. Neither moved.

Finally, his voice barely audible above the noise in the moving branches and squawking wildlife above, Gage said, "I don't understand this attraction between us."

Jennifer swallowed, having hoped that what she was feeling and experiencing had been one-sided and if it wasn't, she hadn't wanted to hear it admitted to out loud. But now that the words were out, they could not be taken back. What did you say to a confession like that when someone was being so honest?

Honesty was the only answer.

"Neither do I."

He stared a moment longer before his head dipped toward hers.

Jennifer saw the intent in his eyes as his lashes lowered and his lips parted. She longed for his kiss, but she backed off instead.

Gage felt her move and opened his eyes. His hands continued to hold her arms steady so she wouldn't fall while he studied her, his gaze inscrutable. "What's wrong?"

Helplessly she shook her head. "I'm sorry, Gage. God is first in my life. He has always been first and I won't risk that when I'm not sure where you stand."

She could have mentioned that he didn't trust her, or that they had problems between them, but she recognized the bigger problem of where his heart was with God. If he couldn't learn to put God first no other problem mattered because a relationship between them would be doomed before it ever began.

Her heart ached as he simply stood there staring. But when he turned and made his way out of the mud, her heart fell to her feet. She was only glad she'd made that statement now, before things went further. At least now, he knew where she stood.

Without a word, he went back to the trail and waited. Jennifer was able to slog her way out this time. She was more careful, imitating the way Gage had gotten out. She knew he'd hear her if she fell and knew he'd come for her. Yet she was glad she didn't have to call out to him again.

When she made it to the trail, he continued on down the path without looking back, somehow making sure the branches never hit her or knocked her down as they went.

No matter how upset he was at her statement, he was still a gentleman. Which made her like him all the more. She knew better than to care for a man who couldn't even take her to pick up some kids, who cared more about his business than anything else. So, why was he the man she suddenly found that she might be falling for?

"Here."

Startled, Jennifer looked up to see Gage holding another branch back and waiting for her to slip past. "I passed this on the way here. You might want to clean up."

Shocked surprise met her eyes. A small stream ran through the middle of the foliage. Its clear rushing water wasn't really noticeable until you came through the trees and bushes and could see it. Then the sounds became discernible.

Gratefully, she smiled up at Gage. "Thank you."

A battle raged within his eyes. After a moment, he finally glanced down and nodded.

Jennifer walked to the stream and managed to kneel within the cool water rushing past and clean herself up. She heard the splashing behind her and to her right and knew Gage was doing the same thing.

He was done quickly and then took a seat on the shoreline to keep a close watch on the surrounding area.

Finally she was done rinsing her hair and crawled out of the water. She walked over to a grassy area and lay down to drip-dry.

Figuring silence was the best thing, she didn't try to fill it with chatter but simply listened to nature's own song.

Her eyes drifted closed and she smiled at the beauty.

"I'm a Christian," Gage said abruptly.

Jennifer was surprised by his sudden announcement, though his admission caused relief to swamp through her. But she didn't comment.

"Things have happened," he continued, his voice struggling with something that was obviously very unpleasant. "Things from the past. I won't discuss them. I see no need to bare my soul like women expect men to do. Suffice it to say, I've learned that as much as our God loves us, He expects us to go through our trials and tribulations alone. He doesn't intervene. He lets us pretty much experience life as it comes and that's that."

Saddened by his words, but thinking his comments about women were very telling, she said, "I've had a few bad experiences in my life, too. However, I believe God still takes a personal interest. He's there in the morning during prayer, that soft gentle voice. He's there when you're hurting, to comfort you. And He's there when things are going wrong, telling you to hang on and believe. Whether you *feel* Him or not. He's there for you. Sometimes it doesn't seem like it. Especially when things are going wrong, but if you don't believe that, then there's not much hope in serving Him."

She knew Gage heard her words, but he didn't comment. Instead, for a while, he only stared off into the distance.

It didn't surprise her when he changed the subject. "You want to tell me again how those guns got into the plane?"

"I honestly don't know." Jennifer's heart broke at Gage's look. "If I did, I'd tell you. I don't particularly like guns. They make me nervous."

"Smuggling guns has nothing to do with personal feelings. It's about money, Jenny."

She noted the shortened version of her name and wondered if Gage realized what he'd said.

Jennifer didn't comment. Only her mother had called her that. But for some reason, it sounded right coming from him, with his softly accented words. "I know, Gage. All I can say is that I didn't put them there and you're going to have to trust me."

Trust. That word caused a fire in his eyes. But not a good one. It was a fire of torment, of a need to believe but a reason to doubt. "I can't."

Jennifer said softly, "It wouldn't matter what I told you, would it?"

"Jenny, *chérie,* you don't understand. Getting caught smuggling guns would destroy my business. I won't let my business fail."

He didn't say it, but it was pretty obvious to her. That was all he had. Whether by choice or not she couldn't say for sure. But if he'd been hurt like she suspected, then his being alone was probably by choice. "You're hiding behind that, you know."

Coolly, he said, "Whatever my reasons, they're my own."

She nodded. When he stood, she followed suit.

He started back toward the path when suddenly he paused. Jennifer paused, too, wondering what it was that made him stop. Then she heard it. A harsh laugh in the distance.

"They're headed this way. Hurry."

Gage pushed her toward the bushes, the gravity of the situation making itself known in his actions as he firmly and determinedly guided her under the heavy brush.

Gage rolled under after her. Tension kept him stiff against her side as he held the machete close against him. More light was visible this time so Jennifer knew they must be more vulnerable than the last time they'd hidden under the bushes for safety.

"They're looking for rebels," she whispered, overhearing the soldiers as they came into view. "I don't think they're looking for us anymore, just rebels in general."

She continued to listen as the men joked, talked, complained. One stopped and leaned down to fill his canteen. Another propped his rifle against the very tree they'd been lying under and stretched.

"Something about others back the other way searching."

Gage touched her lips to quiet her as the men themselves fell quiet.

Jennifer couldn't figure out why his touch bothered her so. But it did.

The feeling was broken when a branch brushed against her shoulder, distracting her.

Moving closer to Gage, she tried to peek out and get a better look at what the men were doing. Both were murmuring now, talking about what could only be guessed at.

They continued to watch as the two men finally continued on down the river, taking a chance to poke here and there at the brush, doing only half a job at looking for the rebels.

They stayed still a long time, making sure the men were gone before Gage finally rolled back over to look at her.

It was the way his eyes widened slightly that told her all was not right.

"What, what is it?" Jennifer froze, not certain what he saw.

"Now, *chérie,* don't panic, you hear me?"

Tension filled her body and she stiffened automatically. "What?"

But she knew. The branch suddenly moved on her shoulder again.

A whimper escaped her lips.

"Just be still."

The branch slithered toward her collar. Soft,

like a gentle weight it inched its way inside the edge of her shirt. Another whimper escaped her.

Gage raised his hand toward the snake.

The snake touched her skin.

Visions of the little child, covered by snake bites, filled her mind.

She screamed.

The jungle protested the intrusion.

Birds flew, animals overhead screeched. Gage grabbed the snake.

But Jennifer was already out from under the bush and still screaming.

Gage tossed the snake and followed her.

She was in hysterics, jumping up and down, her face as white as a sheet. When she saw him come out from under the bush she ran into his arms, blubbering.

"We don't have time for this. Come on!"

Shouts sounded. The soldiers burst into view just as they dove into the jungle's depths on the other side of the small clearing.

Jennifer's screams turned to whimpers as he dragged her through the thick vegetation. "Oh, no, I'm...so-so-sorry," she stuttered, her residual terror still obvious in her speech and eyes.

"I—I didn't mean..." She pushed forward increasing her speed when he jerked on her arm. "I didn't mean..."

"Not now!"

He should have known something would happen—though it hadn't been on purpose. But he'd let his guard down.

They crashed through the bushes, turning every which way, trying to lose their pursuers, but they couldn't shake them. "They know who we are. They're talking about an award for our capture."

That was just what Gage needed to hear. "Great! That means they aren't going to give up easily."

Grabbing her around the waist he pushed her up a small eroded incline, following behind her, prodding her when she didn't move fast enough.

Another shout sounded. Then a popping noise.

"They're shooting at us!"

"Really? What was your first clue?" Gage drawled, grabbing her arm and starting into the brush again.

"*Ah...no...*" His words stuttered out and he stumbled.

Frantic, Jennifer grabbed at him. "What? What is it?" When he slowed down, she hooked her arm around him and prodded him on. "Are you shot?"

His hands were on his face and he growled out something unintelligible. "My eyes. I can't see...bark from the tree."

There was a pause and then louder, he said, "I can't see!"

Jennifer feared they were sunk.

Chapter Eight

Jennifer felt panic rising. *He couldn't see?* Oh, this was not good.

Trust in me and lean not unto your own understanding.

The soft whisper brought a measure of relief to her panic.

"Come on. Hold on to me."

Anchoring the larger body next to her own, she continued to weave in and out, stumbling and being dragged down several times when Gage tripped and fell.

The shouting could still be heard and the enemy was still continuing toward them. Jennifer refused to give up. She turned, circling back, hoping the *federales* would think, in their panic, that she and Gage wouldn't go back the same direction they'd just flown from.

It worked. Bit by bit, the voices faded. As soon as she was certain those men weren't around, she stopped. She didn't want to run into any more troops in their flight. The area was very rocky. She hoped she might be able to find somewhere to hide.

But first things first.

Gage was still rubbing at his eyes, almost gouging them out in his attempt to clean them.

"Here, sit down."

She guided him to a rock partially covered with moss.

He continued to mutter in his Cajun French and Jennifer was glad it was low enough that she didn't hear it. She wasn't sure she wanted to know what he was saying since he was probably expressing his displeasure.

Quickly snatching up a commandeered bottle from their supplies that they were using as a canteen, she opened it.

Batting his hands away she forced his head back. "Let me rinse them. Just keep your head back."

She poured the water in his eyes.

"Woman, you're trying to drown me!"

"No, I'm not," she argued, prying open the lid of one of his eyes and flushing it again. "But we need to get whatever is in there out!"

Again, she poured water in the other eye, holding it open as she did.

When she was certain they were clean, she sat back. "How do they feel?"

Gage rubbed at his eyes with the heels of his hands. "I feel like I tried to steal third base with my eyes open. How do you think I feel?"

Jennifer moved closer at his words. "Let me look at them. Just move your hands—"

"Don't talk to me like I'm a child." Gage's voice vibrated with his anger and frustration.

Carefully, she touched his cheek, trying to project her concern for him. "It's going to be fine."

He immediately stilled. His muttered words fell off in midstream and then he dropped his hands. "Go ahead. Look."

She forced his squinting eyes open. Dark brown irises were surrounded by bloodshot whites—from all his scrubbing.

Gage pulled back from her touch. "They're burning like crazy."

Jennifer released his head, sliding a hand

down to take his hand. She wasn't going to admit it, but she was scared. Very scared. More scared than she'd been the entire trip. *Please, Father, help me.* "I think you may have scratched your cornea."

"You're a nurse now, too?"

Exasperated, Jennifer scowled. "Fine. Tell me what you see?"

Gage squinted. His gaze wandered, back and forth, not really focusing on one object that she could tell.

"Greens, brown and a big white splotch where you're sitting."

"Well, you've definitely irritated them." She continued to hold his hand, thinking. Finally, tentatively, she said, "When I hurt my eyes they made me wear a patch to hurry along the healing. They said if I didn't wear the patch I could hurt my eyes further."

"We don't have any patches and there's no hospital to go to—as if I would go to one here."

"I'm serious, Gage. You can't see now. What if you strain your eyes more?"

"What do you suggest?"

"Let me bandage them until they feel better."

"Oh great! That's just asking for trouble.

What're you going to do? Guide us out of here on your own?''

Jennifer tried not to show her hurt at his harsh words. She knew he was just as scared as her and feeling impotent at the moment. "We'll take it one step at a time. Right now, I'll find us somewhere to hide and who knows, maybe by tomorrow you'll be fine again.''

Gage's face showed his repressed rage in the rigid set of his jaw as he fought the inevitable. "I don't *trust* you,'' he finally said.

There was no way she could dispute the hurt this time as she jerked against his hand. She swallowed once, and then again against the bitter pain his words caused. He had no reason to trust her. She'd failed before. What was to say she wouldn't fail him? But she wasn't going to tell him that. "I don't see as you have any choice.''

She grabbed his backpack, pulling it off his back and then rummaged through it until she found the first aid kit. Pulling out a roll of gauze she wrapped it around his head, over and over until she had a good three-inch circle around his head, completely covering his eyes.

"You don't leave my side, *chérie*, understand?''

"I'd never leave your side, Gage." Her reply came out soft, gentle. "Now, come on."

Slipping the backpack on his back, she helped him stand and then grabbed her own pack. Jennifer guided his arm around her shoulders before sliding her own arm around his waist.

"See if you can find a cave, or maybe a small overhang. It needs to be well disguised, where it won't likely be spotted, somewhere that we can hole up—"

"Gage."

His lips tightened but he stopped his flow of words.

"I know it'd be useless to tell you not to worry, so I won't. However, I will tell you that you don't have any choice—even though that's obvious, too. So, let's just make the best of this."

Gage didn't reply but he did follow as she started walking. As a matter of fact, though he said not a word, his tight grip on her shoulder as he took each step told her how scared he was.

But Gage would never admit it. Men just didn't admit things like that.

"Careful here...."

He stepped in an uneven spot and jerked her

with him. Jennifer's free arm shot out around his waist as she pulled back.

"This isn't going to work."

Angry, Jennifer retorted, "It would if you'd stop being so stubborn!"

Gage paused and his lips parted slightly. Then a slow, reluctant grin turned up the corners of his lips. "The rose has thorns."

"Oh, please...no rose jokes. I've heard them all."

Gage relaxed and Jennifer sighed in relief. "You wouldn't believe how many times and how many different variations."

Jennifer kept up the line of chatter as she deftly led Gage through the thick jungle. It was rougher going than normal, trying to hold on to him and watch all of the branches, but they managed.

After two hours, though, Jennifer was exhausted and had to stop.

"Where are we?"

Jennifer looked up at Gage where he sat propped against a tree. Sliding down next to him she sighed. "I tried to lead us around in a large circle. We're less than a mile or so from the river, somewhere near the mud hole."

"You brought us back?"

"You don't have to sound so shocked. I thought they wouldn't think to look back here for us."

"Of all the..." Gage trailed off and sighed wearily. "I don't know if that's such a good idea. I would imagine the river will draw the soldiers to it."

"Just give me a minute to rest and then we'll go on. I thought we could backtrack a bit and maybe find a cave."

"What? Not leading me to the mission?" he asked sarcastically.

She chuckled. "After we get some rest."

His mouth tightened and she smiled sadly. "Now you know how I feel, Gage, being ordered around and not given a choice."

They both fell silent. Jennifer thought about all that had happened today, the chase, the reason for the chase, her actions. Finally, with a sigh, she said, "I need to apologize for my actions earlier."

The sound of the wind was loud as it rustled through the overhead trees; flapping wings and other wildlife echoed occasionally. Jennifer saw the many different flowers, profuse in the colors of the rainbow and wondered how many dangers hid behind each one.

"You still say you aren't scared of snakes?"

She didn't want to get into this. But she had opened the subject and he had a right to know. "I wouldn't say scared, exactly," she began.

"You can say that. Terrified would be a better description."

"Not terrified, either. I just..." She thought how to tell him what bothered her about snakes. "I have nightmares about them, killing someone."

Gage was quiet for a long time. Finally he asked, "Did it really happen? Was someone you knew killed?"

Very softly, she whispered, "Yes."

She felt his arm go around her shoulders. The gentle acceptance without any demands was surprising and made her want to confess the entire story to him.

Wearily she found herself laying her head on his arm. The width of his shoulder easily supported its weight and its solidity restored her strength. Silently she sat there, absorbing the calm reassurance that radiated from him.

"You should have told me, *chérie*."

"I couldn't."

No words passed again for a short time before he finally said, "I suppose we have both been rather stubborn in our need to have our own way, which has caused us not to depend on each other."

"I suppose so," Jennifer agreed.

"It looks like the choice of depending on each other has been taken out of our hands."

Jennifer chuckled. "Do you mean to tell me you think God allowed your eyes to get hurt so that we'd have to come to grips over helping each other?"

She could see the struggle on his face. "Whatever. It happened and now we have to work together." A loud sigh escaped his lips. "So, what do you suggest we do next?"

A heavily accented voice replied, "I suggest, *señor,* that you be very still and stand. That is what I suggest."

Gage stiffened. Jennifer jerked but saw the cold barrel of a rifle that slipped between them and rested at the base of Gage's neck.

She followed the black metal barrel up its length to see one of the *federales* who had been chasing them earlier grinning from ear to ear.

Chapter Nine

"**W**hat's going on?"

Gage shifted next to Jennifer and she gently laid her hand on his shoulder. "We're at some sort of campsite. We're sitting near a tree." Jennifer glanced at Gage's bound hands and sighed. "At least they haven't bound your feet or tied me up. I guess you look too helpless and I look too terrified."

She laughed nervously.

Gage muttered under his breath. "How many other soldiers are here?"

"Four. The two who brought us and two others. But I count two vehicles and it looks like they're waiting for more people to arrive."

Jennifer studied the men who were currently gambling and drinking, laughing uproariously as they wagered their money and other valuable objects. One, easily twice the size of Gage, spit then wiped at his mouth before glancing their way.

Jennifer admitted she was thoroughly intimidated by them. She and Gage had been poked and prodded and shoved all the way here by the two other men. The fat one and the skinny little bandit, as she thought of him, had already been in camp when they showed up. And now, for the last hour, she had had to listen in lurid detail to what they planned for her and Gage later when *everyone* arrived back at camp.

Gage shifted for what had to be the fifteenth time in the last ten minutes and asked, "What are they saying now?"

Jennifer sighed. She listened. "About the award money and more about...tonight."

Gage's jaw tightened and his hands fisted. Seeing the large *federale* staring their way, Jennifer touched Gage's arm. "They're looking this way."

"We'll get out of here. I'm not going to let anything happen to...us."

Jennifer found she could actually smile. "This

might seem odd, Gage. But I think God has a plan and we're going to be okay.''

Gage's mouth twisted. ''Well, while you're waiting, we need to make plans, too.''

Jennifer sighed. Finally, she turned to Gage. ''Gage, do you think I got us into this mess on purpose?''

Jennifer thought back again to when the soldiers had first found them. Gage had been so quiet, uncharacteristically so. That he blamed her had been one of her secret fears. Gage certainly didn't trust her. With him unable to see, he might not believe anything she was saying. Jennifer shifted, feeling a trail of sweat roll down her back and soak into her shirt as she waited for him to answer.

Gage's mouth turned down a bit at the corners before he finally sighed. ''No. I don't think you had anything to do with this. I don't know why, but I believe you. That's probably going to be my downfall.''

Though he sounded disgruntled, she felt they had just made some progress. ''Do me a favor, then. Continue to act helpless and maybe we can figure a way out of this.''

''I *am* helpless.'' Gage wiped his cheek against his shoulder, swiping at the perspiration, a gesture that only showed how helpless he was to even reach up and dab at his face.

Jennifer chuckled at the thought, because Gage tied was anything but helpless to her. "You're not acting that way. You're bristling even now. If you end up getting your feet tied, then we're out of luck—we'll have nothing. Right now, though, they seem to consider us no threat. I mean, look…er…sorry. What I meant was, our backpacks are within reach. The only thing they took was your machete."

"Which means they're idiots."

"It just means they don't think we can do anything about the situation we're in."

Jennifer shifted and wiped discreetly at her neck and chest. "It's stifling. Maybe the heat is affecting them, too, and that's why they aren't thinking right." She paused. "Uh-oh."

"What?" Gage questioned, hearing a new tension in Jennifer's voice.

"The soldier. The big one. He's looking this way again and getting up."

Gage strained to hear but could distinguish nothing over the regular sounds of the jungle. "Tell me what's going on. Take these bandages off, Jennifer. I need to see."

"No…don't…" Jennifer's strained voice

came to his ears from his left. He heard her cry out and the muffled sound of a struggle peppered with Spanish.

He tried to lunge toward Jennifer when large beefy hands closed around him and hauled him up. "Jennifer? Jenny!"

"I'm okay. He wanted you." She was breathless but sounded okay.

A rapid-fire question was shot at him in Spanish. Gage didn't know what his inquisitor said. He only picked out *gun* and *aeroplane* in the dialogue. "I don't understand you, you big... oooaf."

Gage doubled over in agony at the punch to the gut. Fire spread in his stomach and he was afraid he was going to be sick.

Jennifer cried out but his mind was so filled with pain he couldn't call to her to see what had happened.

The question was repeated. And again the punch to the gut. This time he was certain he was going to lose the little food he had.

Jennifer again cried out. Her voice spit out a quick string of Spanish and then the man holding him growled back. Jennifer replied.

Gage was dropped.

Lying there gasping for breath, he heard her

cry out again and then heard the sounds of a struggle.

"Jenny!" He surged to his knees, feeling rage at how helpless he was.

Then suddenly she was at his side, crying, rattling off sentences at the guard as she held Gage.

"Are you okay?" he demanded, fearful. He'd never heard Jennifer in such a state.

Her arms squeezed him as she continued to utter short, emotion-packed sentences.

A coarse laugh from the soldier told Gage the man was retreating.

"Answer me, Jenny. Are you okay?"

Close to his ear, Jenny whispered. "I'm fine. I just had to convince them I was scared out of my wits. They thought we were planning something and wanted to make sure we understood the error of our ways."

Her words did not reassure Gage. "What happened? What did he do to you?"

Jennifer continued to hold him against her. He could feel her heart rate beating double time. Her embrace comforted him, but the trembling of her hands as she gripped his arms gave her away.

"He just wanted to prove he had control over the situation."

"Jennifer. I have an active imagination. Tell

me it's not as bad as it sounds.'' His voice shook with frustration.

"He only groped me and tried to kiss me. Are you satisfied?"

She pushed away and he realized she was embarrassed.

Gage did his best to control his rage. She didn't need it. She needed his comfort. He leaned back until he found the tree behind him. "Come here, *chérie*. Lean on me for a while."

He heard movement and then she was snuggling up against him. Her head nestled against his shoulder. A shuddering sigh escaped her.

His heart melted.

Every instinct within Gage told him not to go down the road he was going, but it was too late. He cared for this woman, Jennifer Rose. She was unlike anyone he'd ever met before. And as she leaned there against him, drawing strength to endure the next round of whatever they faced, he realized he had never met a woman with the courage this woman had.

Laying his head to the side, he stroked the top of her head with his chin. "Shhh, now, *chérie*. All will be okay. We'll see to it. Don't you worry."

A round of laughter burst from the guards across the compound and he grimaced.

"I'm okay, Gage. Really. I just...thank you for being here. I am sorry that we got into such a mess."

"We'll get out of it. Don't worry."

"You. Woman."

Gage stiffened. So did Jennifer.

"Yes?"

"Is true the cross you wear?"

Jennifer looked up to see two soldiers standing over them.

"What is he talking about?"

She fingered the small cross pendant at her neck. "My necklace."

The guard jerked her up and Gage stiffened. "No, Gage," Jennifer warned. "Just wait."

The other soldier pulled out a gun and cocked it, causing Gage to go very still. "Please, Gage. Trust God. Trust me."

Gage didn't answer but she could tell by the look on his face he didn't like the idea that she was being hauled off. She went with the soldier across the compound to the other man who hadn't approached them yet. "You are a *religioso* then?" he asked in Spanish.

One of the two men to capture them asked her

the question. Jennifer tried not to quiver in fear. Stories of all the tortures and deaths of missionaries ran through her mind, though. She lifted her chin. "Yes. Yes I am," she replied in Spanish. "My friend and I are here to visit Lahara. Our plane went down."

He eyed her speculatively. His eyes kept wandering back to the cross. "Your Lahara. It has helped my sister. It's a good place."

Jennifer relaxed slightly. "Very good."

"But that doesn't explain the guns."

Jennifer looked helplessly at the hardened warrior before her, knowing that they fought against the rebels and were determined in their fight to stop the arms flow into their country. But what could she say? *Father, please help me.* "We don't know about them, either, *señor.* We only know that they are there and that someone else loaded them."

The man studied Jennifer before his gaze dropped to the cross around her neck. Finally, his eyes lifted, a cynical world-weary look deep within them. "I do not believe these words of yours, but you will have protection until our leader returns and we can speak with him."

Thank you, she whispered silently.

He nodded to the other soldier. The soldier

scowled but escorted her back to where Gage sat, the third *federale* still holding a gun to his head.

"Jenny?"

Jennifer sagged down in relief, thinking his abbreviated use of her name never sounded so nice.

"I'm fine. They wanted to know who I was, why I wore a cross around my neck. When I told them I was on the way to the mission they relented."

Gage scowled.

"Honest, Gage. They did." She reached out and touched his arm. "They also asked about the guns. I told them we weren't responsible for them. They didn't believe me, but they're going to wait until the others show up before they question us more."

"Get these bandages off my eyes. I want to see what's going on."

Jennifer sighed. "If I try to take those off, Gage, not only will those men stop me, but they'll start looking at you as a much more dangerous threat. Please, just wait and let's see what happens."

"There's something you're not telling me from earlier, isn't there?"

Jennifer turned, surprised, wondering how he'd known. "Why do you say that?"

"You forget, *chérie,* I understand a few words. And those words I understood was that we'd be better off dead."

Jennifer sighed, having hoped he'd missed that.

"Well?"

"You're right. One of the men said we'd be better off dead, that way the government would still pay the reward money for the rebel trash even though we were Americans. He said he thought the leader would feel that way, too. However, the other one who was with him just promised us safety until the leader arrives."

Gage muttered under his breath—again in his own language.

"Do you know, every time you get really upset, you begin muttering in Cajun French?"

Gage paused and tilted his head. "Old habit I suppose. In Korea, it was easier to work out my problems when no one else could understand what I was saying."

Despite the seriousness of the situation, she chuckled. "Don't I know it."

Jennifer stretched out by Gage, leaning over against the same tree, careful not to give the soldiers any reason to come over and check to see what she was doing. "Well, we'll just sit here and rest until an opportunity presents itself for escape."

Jennifer glanced up at the nearby guard and tried to look wary. It wasn't too hard. Leaning over against Gage slightly, she whispered, "And as long as that guard stands there I don't have much chance of freeing you from these bonds."

Gage stiffened.

"You didn't think I was totally helpless, did you?"

A small smile curved Gage's mouth. "You know, *chérie,* I'm beginning to think I've misjudged you in more than one area."

Jennifer closed her eyes, enjoying the strong comforting feel of his shoulder beneath her cheek.

Nothing else was said as they sat and waited for something to happen.

From under her lashes, Jennifer watched the guards move around as the sky grew darker.

Voices sounded in the distance and then closer. "The leader," she whispered.

"I'm sorry, *chérie,*" Gage replied and Jennifer knew it was concern for her that prompted his words. "Now will you take these bandages off and give us a fighting chance?"

Instead of answering, Jennifer prayed. "Father, please help us. Get us out of this mess. Time is running out."

Gage heard and started. She was praying. Jenny was praying! Right now, when the leader was going to come back and probably order their executions. "Jenni—" he began, only to be brought up short by the sound of a gun blast, very near.

Loud shots and gunfire exploded around him. It sounded like the entire clearing had just erupted into World War III.

Jennifer suddenly gripped Gage's arm as a loud thud sounded near him. "Oh, my word! Rebels are storming the camp! The *federales* are under attack!"

Chapter Ten

Jennifer grabbed both backpacks and urged Gage to his feet. "Come on."

She shrugged one pack onto her back and carried the other. With her free hand, she took hold of Gage.

"Hurry. I don't think they saw us leave."

Bushes slapped him in the face, startling him. Slipping on the soft mushy floor he turned his ankle. He felt totally helpless, unable to put his hands out for protection.

Suddenly Jenny grabbed him. "Down on your knees. We'll crawl under here, back into the brush and hide."

Gage dropped clumsily to his knees and followed Jennifer's prodding. "Careful, *chérie,* I cannot see. These bandages...oomph."

He lost his balance and landed, with a thud, on his stomach. In the distance gunshots and shouting could still be heard. "We didn't go very far," he gasped out.

"Do you think you could have made it?"

She had a point.

"You know, I'm beginning to think this is going to be my entire experience in this jungle— studying the underside vegetation as we lie around and get all mucked up."

Despite the seriousness of the situation, Gage chuckled. "Ah, *chérie,* if we make it out of here, I'll take you on the town and show you a good time. We'll go to the zoo and the aquarium and out to eat. You'll never have to crawl around in the moist vegetation again."

Jennifer stilled, glancing up at him, wishing she could see through the darkness to examine his expression and figure out just what he meant by that. "It's too dark to go on anyway so we're just stuck here."

Suddenly she remembered that Gage was still tied up. "Your hands! Roll over and let me get them loose."

With a few muttered Cajun phrases, he managed to roll over and she went to work on his bonds. Gage lay perfectly still as she worked. It took several minutes before she finally loosened them enough to remove them. In that time the shooting stopped and the sounds of the fight faded. She was certain the *federales* would be out again looking for them. But right now, with it so dark, it would be a hopeless cause. So, they had at least until morning.

"I need to apologize."

Startled, Jennifer paused at his words. "What for?" She pulled the last of the rope away.

With a groan, he started to stretch his arms. She felt him shift until he was once again facing her. Tension sprang up as she waited, racking her brain for what he might mean.

"You were not in on the gun shipment."

Stunned, her mouth dropped open. What had finally convinced him of her innocence?

"Mind telling me what brought you to that conclusion?" she asked.

"No matter how I thought about it, I just couldn't accept that you were really involved. You just didn't fit the profile of a rebel rouser. I don't know how the guns got on board the plane, but I do believe you had nothing to do with them."

Well, she could be grateful for that. "You're right. I had nothing to do with those guns."

Silence fell. Jennifer reeled over the fact that he had actually apologized to her. She didn't know many men who would apologize when they were wrong. Ben certainly hadn't been that way.

Jennifer moved closer to Gage as the temperature dropped. She enjoyed the silence, feeling more at peace than she had all day.

"Why don't you finish telling me the entire story about the snakes?"

The soft words, spoken so gently, undid her completely. She hadn't confided her fears to anyone. Alone in the world as she was, she didn't have anyone to tell, anyone she really trusted. But his voice tempted her, begged her to confide.

Tired of holding it in, she decided to take him up on his request. In the dark where neither could see the other, an air of anonymity pervaded. "My mother operated a day care center. I helped her."

Jennifer's mind drifted back to those days as a child. "You remember me telling you one of the parents taught me the local French. Well, another tutored me in math when I needed it. It was a trade-off for the tuition the parents couldn't afford to put out for their child's day care. My mother was always doing things like that. She loved those kids and thought that the children should have a chance, their parents should have a chance when things were so expensive.

"Needless to say, the day care flourished under my mother's attention.

"I loved being part of my mother's work. I even started dating a guy in school who thought it was cool that I actually was part owner in my mom's business even though I was still so young. You see, my mom added my name to the sign out front, which made it really special for me."

Jennifer sighed. "But then she died."

Sorrowful memories of her mother's death and all the arrangements for the funeral returned. "I was so alone, so...lost, so empty. I didn't have anyone to really help me with funeral preparations, except my pastor. The church ladies all fixed food and clucked over me. But there was no family left since my father left when I was a baby."

Gage's arm stole around her and pulled her close. Jennifer reveled in the closeness. Bitter memories followed as she remembered why it'd been so long since anyone had comforted her. "I turned to my boyfriend for help. His family was one of the more affluent in town and I thought he would have the contacts I'd need to keep the day care open. I thought he could help me when all the parents started pulling their children out because a mere nineteen-year-old was now in charge of the place. And then I couldn't meet the bills.

"My boyfriend insisted the only action was to close the place down. He swore that the parents who had been mooching off my mom's gentle spirit could easily find somewhere else to put their kids. He said his parents gave to several charities and there were all kinds of programs out there that could take care of the kids."

Her voice dropped. "I wanted to believe him so it's just as much my fault. And at the time I hadn't realized how demanding and selfish his reasons were for me to get rid of the day care. Looking back, I realize it always had to be his way or no way. And I was young enough, stupid enough, to let him have his way."

Jennifer shook off the pain. "Anyway, I closed the doors of the center, though I didn't forget the children as easily. There were these three families who couldn't afford day care and couldn't find anywhere to keep their kids. By now I was having financial troubles, having to sell my mom's house and move and try to pay some of the debts I didn't know my mom had. I couldn't watch the kids like I wanted to. But I knew these families were leaving their kids home alone. One family in particular really worried me. There was a nine-year-old, a four-year-old and a fifteen-month-old.''

Jennifer shuddered as the nightmare surfaced in her mind. Determinedly she tried to push it away but it wouldn't be banished as again it replayed itself in her mind. Chills worked their way up from her depth, causing her voice to shake even as goose bumps broke out on her arms.

''Shhh, *chérie*. It'll be okay.'' Gage moved his rough, calloused hand up and down her arm, his words soft. But his touch did no good. Jennifer was still chilled to the bone.

''This particular morning I had just finished moving into a small apartment and decided to go pick up some breakfast for the kids. Sherri, Martine and Bebe, as they called Matt, rarely got fast food and I wanted to surprise them with breakfast.''

Jennifer's voice dropped, low and strained as she continued. ''I went to the house to find the kids. Sherri wasn't at home, I later found out. She'd spent the night with a friend but had promised her mom to be home by seven. She'd overslept. That's why when I arrived at ten, no one answered the door.

''Since her mom had to go into work at six, she'd left the kids asleep thinking her older daughter would be home within the hour.''

''She was comfortable leaving a nine-year-old in charge? But that's so young.''

Jennifer shrugged. ''People do it all the time. Single mothers who just can't make a living and pay for child care. Anyway, I could hear Bebe crying and so I went on in. It wasn't until I came to Martine's room and saw Bebe sitting by his sister who looked to be still asleep that I had an inkling something was the matter.''

Gage suddenly stiffened, knowing what was coming. ''A snake?''

''Uh-huh. Evidently it had crawled into the bed and bit her in the neck during the night. She'd been bitten four times. She was probably dead when the mother left. Her body was cold. It was...swollen,'' she whispered. ''I don't know how Bebe managed not to get bitten. I called an ambulance. The snake was discovered in the closet. A copperhead. Evidently it had crawled into the bed for warmth, the medical worker said. Every time the child moved, the snake bit her."

"Oh, Jenny, *chérie,*" Gage whispered, pulling her close. This woman was a survivor. "It's not your fault." Gently, he stroked her hair.

"It was my fault. If I hadn't given in and listened to my boyfriend, maybe I could have still been watching those kids—"

"No, *chérie.* You said you were having financial problems. There was no way you could have stayed in business once you lost your clientele."

"I don't know. But I do know I'm not going to let any child be endangered—if I can help it. That's why I must get to Lahara."

He wanted to take her pain away. But he was afraid he had nothing to really give her.

"Jenny, do you realize if you go on to the mission the *federales* will find us? You told them where we were headed."

"I'm going to get those kids, Gage. I *have* to get them. Especially now, if the *federales* decide to pay the mission a visit."

Gage hugged her, laying his head against her

head. "It's not possible, *chérie*. I won't let you go and get hurt."

Jennifer struggled against him. "Why, Gage? After disbelieving every word I said, sneering at my explanations, it makes no sense that you would suddenly worry about me."

Gage stiffened, but knew her anger was justified. How could he explain his sudden mixed emotions for the beauty before him? Should he tell her he found her courageous and special, that he cared what happened to her? Despite his better judgment about ever getting involved with someone, Jennifer had wormed her way into his heart.

It wasn't love. He didn't believe in love anymore. But he did care for her. Too much.

No, he wouldn't tell her of his feelings and let her use them as a weapon against him.

Instead, he replied, "Hey, anyone would care what happened to another person. I can accept you didn't have anything to do with the guns. But someone did, and I have to get back, get in touch with my partner and have him start looking into the situation before whoever is guilty can cover their tracks."

Jennifer sighed. "Well, fine. Then if that's the way it's going to be…"

She shouldn't be surprised he would talk to her like that. He'd made it clear his business came first. She just kept forgetting. Her feelings were once again getting in the way of her common sense.

"Jennifer?" Gage's hand stopped her as she tried to move away. "Don't be angry, *chérie*."

She sighed. "I'm not." And she wasn't. Disappointed, but not angry.

His hand moved up over her face, cupping her cheek. His lips found hers in a gentle kiss.

Surprised, Jennifer didn't respond at first. But she liked it and leaning forward, she allowed the tender embrace.

Then it was over.

"We'd better get some sleep." His tone of voice told her he had been affected as much as she, but he wouldn't admit it.

Jennifer was tired, though, of letting him get away without ever answering a question. Deciding to try to pin him down about his feelings, she asked, "Why did you kiss me?"

There was a pause, and then his voice, so soft that she almost missed it, replied, "Because you're just too good to be true."

Well, it wasn't a confession, but it healed Jennifer's hurt feelings. Silently she prayed to God and mentioned to Him that if this was the man He had picked out for her, then He was going to have to do some healing and changing to both of their hearts.

Chapter Eleven

"So, how are they?"

Gage peered blearily ahead, squinting into the early dawn. Large green-and-brown shapes blurred together along with the white form of Jennifer. "Well, I can see some, though it's still a bit blurry. But it doesn't matter. I'm not putting those bandages back on for anything."

"I can't tell you how good it is to hear that."

He could make out Jennifer's small smile.

"Here. I found some fruit on a nearby tree. Eat this."

Gage squinted at what she handed him. Berries and some nuts. "Thanks."

He popped them in his mouth, starved. "Any

sign of the *federales?*'' Carefully he stood, then finished off the small amount of food she'd provided.

''Not a sign. If they came this way, we slept through it.''

Gage nodded. Looking both left and right he tried to decide which way to head.

''We came from that way.'' Jennifer pointed toward the south. ''The path is a few hundred yards over there. It's a pretty wide path, like an overgrown road.''

''It probably is.'' Gage slowly traversed the bushes, grabbing Jennifer's hand and pulling her after him. ''They have a lot of villages out in the jungles. The roads are for those few who own vehicles as well as the gunrunners, rebel fighters and police. Let's get back to it and follow it. Hopefully, it'll lead us somewhere.''

Though Gage was certain Jennifer could make it on her own, he liked holding her hand. It was soft, gentle, small in his bigger one. He found he didn't want to let go, and...for the first time, ignored the inner warning and did what he wanted.

Last night things had shifted and changed. His world had tilted on its axis. Though he still didn't trust her, because he doubted any woman knew her own heart and would be totally truthful with him, he could admit now that he would like to get to know Jennifer better.

He didn't have to love her to get to know her. And he could—emotionally—keep her at a distance while still getting to know her.

Realizing how cynical that sounded, he thought maybe Jennifer was right when she hinted that he put too much emphasis on his anger and fear to trust anyone. It bothered him a bit that she had figured that out. Oh, she hadn't come right out and accused him of being afraid to trust. But he'd gotten the gist of it from their discussions.

"See, this is what I was talking about."

Gage looked around and saw a beaten-down path, worn by trucks that had probably passed through on a fairly regular basis. "I'd say your sight is very astute. This is definitely a road."

Gage pulled her closer to stand beside him before he started walking again. Her companionship was something he found himself enjoying as they walked down the overgrown path without fighting the bushes and underbrush. A loud chattering above brought both of their heads up.

Jennifer chuckled. "From what I've read, there are other animals we haven't seen yet. The missionaries mentioned a margay, sorta like a jaguar or something.''

Gage chuckled. ''Yeah. I don't think it's going to bother us.''

Jennifer shrugged. ''If you say so. But there are still other animals. I wonder if we'll see a tapir. It supposedly lives in the jungles.''

Gage thought of the animal that looked like a cross between a pig and an anteater and smiled. ''Let's hope not. And let's hope those howler monkeys don't give our position away.''

He hurried her on, leaving the noisy monkeys behind. ''You know, if I still had my machete, we might just have a tapir or something else to eat.''

''The berries weren't enough, were they?''

Gage squeezed her hand. ''Let's just keep a watch out for any other fruit or nuts along the road.''

All was peaceful as they continued on quietly hand in hand, following the trail, looking much like a couple out on a date. Except that both Gage and Jennifer were bruised and scratched and hadn't had a decent bath with real soap in two days. But Gage didn't mind. He simply continued to walk in the silence, enjoying the profuse beauty around him as well as the beauty next to him as they covered each additional mile.

"Gage?" Jennifer broke the silence.

"Hmmm?" he replied, still caught up in the lovely scenery.

"Tell me about your family."

Gage's tranquil state suddenly shattered at her words. "My family?"

This time it was Jennifer who squeezed his hand. "I was curious. I know you have a sister."

Gage sighed. *Women.* They were always curious.

He had to admit, though, after all the questions he'd asked her, all the accusations he'd hurled at her, she had a right to ask some questions of her own.

He thought about his sister, back home. His jaw softened just the tiniest bit as he began to speak of Rebecca. "Becca is a bit younger than me. She's a tomboy, has always been a tomboy. She's married and has three kids but is *still* a tomboy. If it weren't for the help her husband gives her around the house, I think her house would stay an utter mess, just like her disorganized mind."

"Gage!"

Gage chuckled. "It's a long-standing feud between us. She drives me crazy and I harass her about her forgetfulness and her utter lack of femininity. I don't know that I ever see her in a dress unless her husband asks her to wear one.''

''Well, maybe some women just don't like dresses.''

Gage turned a small grin down to his T-shirt clothed companion. ''Is that so?''

Jennifer smiled archly, ''That's so. And I think your sister deserves a break about that.''

Gage chuckled. ''Don't worry. Her husband doesn't force her to do or wear anything she doesn't want to. I imagine if she wanted to run around in her pajamas he would let her, she's got him so wrapped around her little finger.''

''Gage!''

He chuckled again. ''Calm down. I was only kidding. Anyway, Becca has an almost three-year-old boy and a one-year-old set of twin girls. They keep her hopping.''

''I imagine. What does your mother think of them?''

Gage frowned, his good humor deserting him. ''My mother fell ill and died when Becca was planning her wedding.''

''Oh, Gage. I'm so sorry.''

"Don't be. She died thinking both of her children were to be happily married."

Too late Gage realized what he'd said. Warily, he glanced down at Jennifer hoping she'd missed the reference. Of course, she hadn't. The woman didn't miss anything.

"I take it things didn't work out between you two?"

"No. You could say that."

He could feel her eyes on him though he stared straight ahead, keeping an eye open for holes as they traversed the uneven ground. Of course, it was too much to hope she wouldn't ask why. And maybe he was glad. That way everything could be out in the open and she could finally see why, though he liked Jennifer, nothing between them could develop further.

"She hurt you?"

Gage laughed mirthlessly. "You could say that, too. I was in the army, stationed in Korea for a year. Angela wanted to wait until I returned to get married. We both agreed it'd be better that way. Becca was going to have a long engagement. She was only barely seventeen and my mother wanted her to wait until she was at least eighteen to make sure she knew what she was doing. Robert was twenty-three, you see. Angela insisted it'd be so romantic if we married on the same day as my sister.

"My sister felt the same way. Unfortunately, during this time my mom fell ill."

Jennifer slid her arm around Gage's waist and hugged him gently before loosening her hold on him. Gage, however, allowed his arm to drift around her shoulders. The contact felt good as he relived the difficult memories.

"What happened? Did you get home early to see your mom and discover your fiancée was dating someone else?"

"No. I had no idea my mom was sick or what Angela was doing. You see, Robert and Becca got so caught up in helping take care of Mom that they didn't realize Angela was seeing someone else. She just stopped coming around as Mom got worse. It wasn't until my mother died that Becca realized what was happening."

Gage sighed, looked at the sky, blinking back the unaccustomed sting in his eyes. "No one bothered to tell me my mother was dying until it was too late."

Jennifer stumbled, whether at his words or because of the uneven ground he wasn't sure. He grabbed at her to keep her from falling, then continued to hold her tightly against him as the old sorrow washed through his body.

Her arms went willingly around him, holding him close in return. Harshly, he continued. "My sister and mother lied to me the entire time I was in Korea. They never once hinted, in any of their letters, that Mom was ill. She just kept telling me that God took a personal interest in my life and to trust Him. It wasn't until Robert wrote me on the sly and asked me about possibly returning early that I had any inkling something wasn't right. But by the time I got his letter a friend of mine was on trial and I couldn't leave because I was implicated along with him. It took me two weeks to get everything cleared with the courts before I could get back home and then it was just too late."

Jennifer held on to him tighter.

"I'd been worried sick about a friend of mine. I found out he was illegally selling guns and munitions on the black market. I was so involved in trying to get him out of trouble that I didn't realize someone was already investigating him. My friend, in a panic, planted papers in my locker to shift the blame. But it wasn't until he was shot and killed that the military intelligence closed in and made the arrests.

"Had my mother or sister hinted that Mom was ill, I would have put in for emergency leave and I probably never would have ended up having to defend myself in court and take down the memory of my best friend at the same time."

A deep shuddering sigh escaped him and then he whispered, "And I would have gotten to see her alive one last time, to apologize for insisting on going in the army when I knew she didn't want me to."

Slowly, he got himself under control, released her and began to walk again.

"And you blame God?" she asked when he continued down the road without saying anything.

Gage shrugged. "Mom was a strong Christian. She believed God took a personal interest in our lives. She taught us to believe that, as well. But I don't see how God watched over me in Korea."

Jennifer realized they were at the crux of Gage's problem. Gage was bitter that everyone betrayed him at once and felt guilty for not being there for his mother. "What happened with Angela?"

Gage shrugged. "When I got home for

Mom's funeral I found out she was going to marry an old friend of mine within the week.''

"She never wrote you?"

Gage shook his head.

Jennifer was appalled, thinking that someone would actually do that to another person.

No wonder Gage didn't trust anyone. He was so bitter, thinking no one cared at all, or probably could ever care for him. *Father, he is hurting so much. Tell me what to do, what to say.*

"Sometimes," Jennifer began carefully. "We don't understand why things happen the way they do and it's easy to blame God for those problems. But, Gage, it's possible that God allowed the events for a reason."

Gage snorted. "He allows them to happen, Jenny, or he just doesn't care to stop them."

Jennifer squeezed his hand. "If you hadn't gone to Korea, if you had come home, then maybe the person in Korea would have died without a second chance and finding the Lord. Maybe you would have ended up marrying Angela and now be divorced, or any number of other things. We can't second-guess God."

Gage increased the tempo of his stride. "I'm not second-guessing God. It's simple to me. God provided a way of salvation. But that was His job for us. He expects us to do everything else on our own.''

Jennifer hurried to keep pace with Gage. "He gave man woman so that they might cling together. That doesn't sound like doing things alone to me.''

Gage slowed without looking at her. Jennifer was rather glad he didn't glance down, though, because his jaw was rigid. "Well this man was meant to be alone, because I can tell you, Jenny, I will never trust a woman not to put her own feelings first to the point that she'd eventually decide she had better things to do than stick around and work at a marriage.''

Dismayed, Jennifer tried to think what to say. "You can't mean that, Gage.''

Gage finally paused and turned empty eyes to Jenny. "What else am I to believe? Why would I even want to believe and end up hurt again? No, I know that to trust would eventually mean being betrayed.''

Hurting for him, Jennifer responded, "I wouldn't betray you, Gage.''

Gage stared at her. "Didn't you try to sneak off after I had told you we had to go back to the main city?''

Guilt stabbed Jennifer. "But, Gage, those kids need me."

"They have the missionaries. They'll be safe until we get back to the city and get everything straightened out."

"I can't desert them," she whispered, realizing that by making the children her priority, she was putting Gage second.

He realized it, too, as his mouth tightened. Lifting a sardonic brow, he replied, "Then it looks as if we've made our choices."

He started walking again. "And, Jenny, despite what you think, I'm not an ogre. I would have made sure there was someone to take you to the mission after everything was straightened out."

"But *you* wouldn't have?"

He shrugged. "I have to find out about those guns."

Put everything else before anything that might get personal, Gage. Go ahead, but that's not going to stop me from trying to heal that broken heart of yours in the time we have left. Jenny couldn't believe her thoughts. But it was true. He was hurting. He would never put anything personal before his business simply because he'd been burned one too many times.

But maybe she could teach him that God did take a personal interest in him, that He did care what happened to Gage. If she could just do that, then she would accept that Gage wasn't the one for her and go back to her own home and nurse the thought that she could have really enjoyed sharing her life with this man.

Jennifer suddenly wondered when her goal had changed from getting to those kids first to helping this man. Then she realized her goal hadn't changed, but she'd just added another one. Now, instead of three lost, motherless little children who needed love and reassurance she had added to that list one troubled man.

Chapter Twelve

"**W**hat is that?"

Jennifer stopped, almost running into Gage when he halted suddenly. Dazedly she looked around. They'd covered a great deal of ground today. She was hot, tired, and afraid she was a bit dehydrated. Wiping the back of her hand across her salt-encrusted forehead she grimaced. "What was what?"

Gage caught her by the arm to steady her while he listened. Suddenly, Jennifer heard it, too. "Voices."

"Yeah, voices," he muttered and, keeping a firm grip on her arm, eased backward into the brush away from the voices.

Jennifer wished Gage had the machete but knew he wouldn't use it and leave an obvious path, so she forgot the slap and pull of the branches and moved back with him.

"They don't sound like soldiers," Jennifer said softly. "I think those voices belong to children. The *federales* don't bring their families with them."

"But the rebels might," he said.

"And we might just be near a village."

"With our luck?" Gage sent her a telling look.

Jennifer had to admit he was right. But still, if there was a chance help was nearby... Jennifer sank to her knees and crawled through the brush ignoring Gage as he tried to stop her.

Peeking out, seeing no one on the road, she quickly crawled across it and into the other brush, deciding one little peek wouldn't hurt.

"Jenny! Come back here. You'll get us both killed." He quickly crawled to where she'd settled.

"You're going to get us caught if you're not quiet," Jennifer warned, hurrying forward. "You know, Gage, I think I prefer traveling through the jungle on my knees. You don't hit as many branches. Yikes!"

Jennifer smacked her head right into the legs of the very people she was planning to sneak a quick look at.

The boy was just as surprised, letting out a squawk before pointing a rifle at her.

"*¡Hola!*" she said, weakly, trying to smile at the boy.

"*¿Quién ere tu?*" the boy asked, nervously. He swung the gun from her to Gage.

"What's he—?"

"Just be still, Gage. He's a bit nervous."

Gage snorted.

The others, alerted by the boy's shout, were hurrying over. Slowly, Jennifer stood, keeping her hands in sight. She glanced at the women and children, some with guns, others not, and smiled in relief.

No men with patches or chewing tobacco and toting guns in sight. Of course, her idea of rebels might be wrong since she had never actually seen a rebel.

"*Me llamo Jennifer Rose y él es Gage Dalton.*" She motioned toward Gage as she introduced herself and her companion to the boy.

"*¿Qué hacen aquí?*"

Jennifer eased her hands down. "We're here because," she paused, switched to Spanish and continued, *"Nuestro avion..."* She made a motion with her hands like an airplane flying. *"Se estrelló,"* she finished and her hand made a sharp downward motion.

She smiled simply and shrugged, hoping to put them at ease with such a simple explanation.

Turning to Gage she explained. "They wanted to know who we are and why we're here." Smiling again at them, she asked, *"¿Está La Mision Lahara cerca de aquí?"*

The gun dropped and several people started questioning her in rapid-fire succession and telling her where the mission was.

"Sí. Sí. La Mision Lahara está cerca pero los rebeldes y los federales..."

"What are you telling them?" Gage demanded.

Jennifer motioned with her hand for him to wait as she listened to the others speak.

"¿Oh?" She nodded. *"Sí. Sí."* Again she nodded. Finally, she smiled. *"Gracias."*

"Well?" he asked, his arms folded.

She shrugged. "I didn't get many words in edgewise. Pedro here was sent with the women to guard them from the rebels or soldiers that might hurt them while they gathered supplies for a party. Evidently today is the celebration of the island's founding. The local village, about eight hundred or so from what I gathered, are getting ready to have a huge celebration tonight. That's where this road leads, by the way.''

Gage studied her, his eyes narrowed. ''And what was that about Lahara Missions?''

Jennifer smiled sweetly. ''They know where Lahara Missions is from here and will gladly direct us there after the celebration tonight.''

Gage's frown turned foreboding. ''We're not going to Lahara Missions. That would be like walking right into a trap.''

Jennifer shrugged. ''Since I speak Spanish and you don't, it looks like we're going where I say.'' She gave him a bright smile. ''Unless you learn Spanish quickly and can figure out how to change their minds between now and tonight after the celebration.''

''I won't let you do this.''

Jennifer smiled cheekily. ''Too late, I already have. Now come on, let's go enjoy the celebration.''

The women began chattering again, wanting to know if she was from North America or Texas and she told them yes on the first but Louisiana on the second. They wanted to know if Gage was her *esposo*. She was glad Gage couldn't understand their question and she told them no, he wasn't her husband. She explained the trip she was on and why and the women empathized because many of them had experienced loss in their own families.

By the time they reached the village, Gage was seething and Jennifer was gloating and she and the women were best friends.

"They've offered us baths and clothes, which I suggest you don't turn down at the risk of offending them."

Gage shot her a look. "Of course I wouldn't offend them."

The village was fairly large, surprising Jennifer. The buildings all had thatched or tin roofs and varied in size.

Children ran around barefoot playing games while men and women hurried back and forth preparing for the festivities.

Boards were being set up along one side of the main square and she found out this was for the food everyone would bring to the celebration.

The woman leading them motioned them across the compound to a younger lady. After a quick exchange the woman turned and spoke to Jennifer.

"She wants us to follow her. She'll take us to a family who can supply us with clothes. Evidently, Lahara does quite a bit of work with them."

"Ask her if they have phones or radios here," Gage said, following along beside Jennifer.

Jennifer repeated the question.

The woman nodded and, with her hands waving as she talked, explained in great detail while Gage bit his tongue.

"Yes, they do," Jennifer finally said. "The church has one. She said after we are done we can go speak with the pastor—"

"Do they have transportation? I'd be glad to pay for gas."

Jennifer sighed and turned back and this time her explanation was very long.

She listened attentively, pausing outside a building when the woman stopped.

Finally, she turned back to Gage. "Yes."

"Yes? Yes what?"

Jennifer smiled. "This is the building where you can bathe. I'll be next door. Yes, they do have transportation. The local pastor here will escort us to the mission—"

"Jenny—"

"Ga-age?" She raised an eyebrow.

He could only steam. Twice he opened his mouth to argue, but finally just turned and went in the building.

"Your man, he is upset."

Jennifer turned in surprise to the young woman named Martina. "You speak English?"

Martina smiled. "*Sí*. I work some at the mission and the missionaries taught it to me. The pastor here, José, we are to be married soon, and he felt it was important we both speak English as well as Spanish, though I know my English is heavily accented."

Jennifer grinned. "Thank you. And again, I really appreciate the offer to bathe."

Martina led her to a small hut for bathing. "Our showers are not as good since we tote the water. But you can dip it out and pour it over you."

"I assure you, anything is better than the state I'm in."

"We do have plumbing we have put in, but it doesn't work much of the time. I will be back shortly with some clothes," the other woman said, leaving.

Jennifer removed her T-shirt and jeans and laid them aside. "This is wonderful," she said out loud as she poured the water over her and soaped her hair.

Jennifer finished bathing and then dried off with the towel Martina had left behind for her.

Wrapped in the towel, Jennifer stepped out of the tiny enclosure and saw that Martina had returned. She held an outfit for her.

"Oh," Jennifer said, looking at the yellow blouse with embroidery around the collar. "That is beautiful. I can't possibly take it."

Martina appeared hurt. "But it is mine. I have many like this. I would give it as a gift of hospitality and for you to wear tonight."

Realizing she shouldn't have refused the clothes, Jennifer backtracked. "I would love to wear it. But, would you think about making a trade?"

She had noted the way Martina had eyed her American clothes with envy and imagined, even if she didn't wear them, she could sell them for quite a bit. "If you give me this to wear, then perhaps you would accept my shirt and jeans in exchange."

Martina's eyes lit up and she smiled. "I would be honored." She picked up the purple-and-yellow shirt. "It is football?"

Jennifer chuckled. "How did you know that?"

Martina beamed. "Americans all wear football symbols. I learned that at the mission."

Jennifer nodded. "Well, yes. It is football. It is a college team in Louisiana."

Reaching for the yellow blouse and matching skirt, Jennifer slipped into them. They were soft, well-worn, but hung beautifully on her. The red, blue, green and brown embroidered flowers along both sides of the neck looked nice against her skin. She quickly tied the strings at the top of the blouse that met just below her collarbone and then reached up to pull her hair back.

"Oh, please, Señora Jennifer, leave it down."

"*Señorita,* Martina," she corrected. With a shrug she allowed Martina to comb her hair for her, leaving it down.

"I insist you allow me to help fix the meal."

"We will see," Martina simply said and then escorted her back outside.

Jennifer opened her mouth to ask Martina another question when she spotted Gage. The words died on her lips.

A loose white shirt, tucked into rough blue drawstring pants that were a tad too short looked good on him despite the length. She couldn't help but grin when she saw he no longer wore work boots but an old pair of canvas shoes.

Martina excused herself in Spanish and then left. Jennifer barely noticed because she was preening under Gage's appreciative look.

Slowly she twirled. "Martina sews well, doesn't she?"

She turned back to Gage. When he didn't comment she hesitated, wondering if she had misinterpreted his look.

Gage moved closer and reached up to softly gather a strand of her hair, rubbing it between his fingers. "Your hair is so beautiful."

Her cheeks heated. Softly, she replied, "Thank you."

Gage lowered his head and Jennifer knew he was going to kiss her. She wasn't sure about the sudden change in him, but she liked it.

Tilting her head she waited. Her eyes drifted shut.

Just as their lips touched, a loud spurt of giggles sounded.

They sprang apart.

Jennifer looked around, surprised by the noise and just a bit disappointed until she saw half a dozen children standing there pointing and jabbering.

A slow smile spread across her face and she leaned forward, putting her hands on her thighs, getting down on level with them.

"¿Qué buscan, niños?" she said, asking the children what they were looking for.

They immediately rushed forward. *"A ustedes señorita y señor."*

"Oooh, bonito," a little girl said touching Jennifer's hair.

In minutes they were surrounded by the children, all of them wanting to touch Jennifer's *blanco* and *amarillo* hair. "I agree that it's yellow, dear ones," she said looking at Gage, "but not *blanco*."

Gage smiled.

Jennifer chuckled. "I'm sure they would understand white if they saw a bleached blonde."

"¿...un beso?"

Jennifer turned to the little girl who was giggling and blushed. "No," she replied, shaking her head and smiling.

Gage, not understanding, glanced at Jennifer. "What?"

She wouldn't meet his eyes, which intrigued him.

"What?" he demanded again his grin spreading when he realized she was embarrassed.

"The little one here wanted to know if you were still going to kiss me. I told her no."

Several of the older children were now commenting on what they'd seen and what the little girl had said as a few of the adults grinned and watched the scene unfolding with indulgence.

Gage winked at the little girl and then smiled at Jennifer. "Well, I don't see why not."

Her face flamed. "Oh, Gage, I don't think so."

He moved toward her, causing the little kids to shriek with delight. A few of the younger men encouraged him while the women prodded at the men to stop teasing.

"Don't do it," Jennifer warned.

Too late she realized she shouldn't have dared him. With a leap, he pulled her into his arms, turning her around and bending her over his arm slightly. "Don't do it?" he mimicked, grinning widely and then before she could stop him, lowered his mouth to hers.

The emotional kiss took them both by surprise. When it was over, Gage pulled back and stared. Jennifer's eyes widened in dismay as she realized being in Gage's company was something she really wanted to continue in her life.

Gage's eyes became inscrutable. Then with a

forced smile he lifted her back up and looked at the children around them.

"Gage...I..."

Gage shook his head. "It was my fault for teasing."

Jennifer's dismay increased. *But you need to tease, to lighten up,* she thought in despair.

It was the first time she'd seen him lighten up and have fun—and then the mood had been ruined when the kiss had turned serious.

She didn't want serious. Serious scared her to death with this man.

He didn't want serious. After all that had happened in his life, serious meant betrayal.

But it looked like neither one of them had much of a choice because Jennifer suddenly realized that she could very easily love this man. Not only that, but she might already be *in* love with this man.

No, no, no. She would not let herself fall in love with him. So what if he had a soft heart underneath all of that pain? So what if he could joke with the kids here? So what if he might even be attracted to her?

He couldn't...wouldn't let go of his hurt and anger against God. A relationship could never survive that.

How did she know he couldn't? Because she was certain one of the main reasons he didn't want to go to the mission was simply because it was one of those places where you had to face God. You had to face that God took a personal interest in your life. And there was no way Gage was going to admit that so he ran, as far and as fast from the mission as possible.

She was certain had his company been able to afford to lose the Richardsons' business he would have backed out of the deal to fly her here.

Nope. She was not going to fall in love with him. No way.

"Let's go help the others," she said, longing for another glimpse of the fun-loving Gage she'd seen minutes ago.

Chapter Thirteen

Jennifer joined the others, only to find most of the cooking had been done. Corn tortillas were laid out in abundance as were beans and *plátanos,* a bananalike fruit that was cut at an angle and then fried. All types of fresh fruits joined the delicious repast. Water as well as other drinks were set upon the table for the thirsty.

Few forks were seen. Jennifer noted most people used their tortillas to scoop up their food once it was on their plate.

"About the radio?" Gage said, reaching for his plate.

Jennifer slapped his hand. "You'll get me in trouble if I let you fix that." She grabbed up one of the chipped pieces of crockery and filled the plate. "Martina is the pastor's fiancée. She said he would be back within the hour. Then you can make your call. But, Gage, let him enjoy the celebration a bit before he takes us to the mission."

Gage growled before saying, "The mission isn't a safe place to go, Jenny. At least go back to town and then you can send a message to the mission."

Jennifer simply smiled, handed Gage his plate and filled her own. "By the way, don't eat any of the fruit that doesn't peel or drink the water unless you want to get sick."

"I know that," Gage replied.

Jennifer shrugged. "Good. Now eat. And smile before they think you aren't enjoying their celebration."

Gage sighed and ate. Jennifer watched, amused, as he devoured his food and went back for seconds.

As she finished her plate of food, musicians struck up an upbeat tune. When Gage came back she mentioned, "One of the women told me the soldiers often come by to participate in these festivals. Also, some of the rebels actually lived

here at one time. If it's clear of soldiers, those
men will usually come to visit relatives.''

Gage paused in his eating. ''Just when did the
woman tell you this?''

Jennifer smiled. ''On the way to camp.''

When his features turned dark she hurriedly
explained, ''I didn't tell you because I knew
you'd react this way. We have to participate or
risk offending these nice people. Besides, what
good would it do to run off now when we will
have an escort soon?''

Gage didn't comment, only continued to
scowl.

Women came and went, speaking to her and
commenting to Gage through her. Most of them
mentioned how much they were enjoying their
guests. Even some of the men came up and
talked with him through Jennifer about America.

Everyone was very curious about America
and *los norteaméricanos ricos*. To them, everyone in America had to be rich. There was money
on the streets for anyone to have, if they could
be believed. And in a way, it was true. At least
Jennifer thought so when she found out Martina's family of thirteen lived in a house the size
of her bedroom back home.

Martina caught Jennifer's eye and motioned

to her. A short thin man in his early twenties, very handsome and earnest looking, stood next to Martina.

Jennifer touched Gage's forearm. "They're here." She nodded to Martina.

Gage relaxed. "Good. Let's go see what we can find out."

They crossed the darkening compound to where Martina and her soon-to-be husband stood.

"*¡Hola! ¿Cómo está?*" Jennifer smiled and stuck out her hand toward Gage. "*Esto*—"

"Please, Señorita Jennifer, I speak English."

Jennifer smiled. "Great."

Gage stuck out his hand. "I'm Gage Dalton. Has Martina explained what happened?"

"*Sí,* Señor Gage. You were in the plane that crashed. The police and the rebels are searching for you."

The pastor no longer smiled, but looked very serious. Gage shot Jennifer an exasperated glance. "That's correct. Unfortunately for us, someone thought to smuggle guns on my plane. I'm trying to get back to the main city of Paulo so I can contact my office to let them know we're all right and see if Sam, my partner, knows what's going on."

The young man studied him for a long time before he finally asked, "You can trust that this Sam is not the one who shipped the guns?"

Jennifer knew it angered Gage to be asked that, but he didn't show it. Instead, he nodded. "It had to be someone else. No one in the business would do this. It's too dangerous."

The young pastor nodded. "These guns, they make our job hard. Many of our men and boys are fighting a useless battle with weapons when they should be on their knees in prayer seeking out answers. The government, it is not so bad. It is the corruption in the *federales* that causes the problems."

He gave a weary smile. "But you do not care of this. You wanted to ask a question?"

Gage nodded, his features carved in grave lines. "Do you have a shortwave we could use?"

Pastor José pursed his lips as he considered the question. "No. I'm afraid ours is broken."

Gage sighed and his shoulders slumped a bit.

"That is where I've been," José continued, noting Gage's reaction and his face registering compassion. "We have very little funds and someone at Lahara is currently working to fix our radio."

José suddenly smiled, his eyes lighting up with an idea. "If you would like, the man who brought us here could give you a ride back."

Gage's smile turned strained. He'd hoped to go on to Paulo instead of the mission compound. He told the pastor of his dilemma.

José nodded again, considering the problem. Finally, he shrugged. "You will need to take that up with him."

José reached out and slapped Gage on the back, ending the conversation. "Now, we celebrate this night. Can I not convince you to stay and share a few more hours with us?"

Gage shook his head. "If the man is going back to the mission now, then we'd better leave."

"Of course." He shook Gage's hand then turned to Jennifer. "I thank you for the exchange of clothes you've given Martina." For the first time, José smiled at Jennifer. "They will bring much to us here."

"I hope so," Jennifer said fervently, deciding to tell her pastor about this young man and the work he did here out in the jungle. She hugged Martina.

"*Vaya con Dios,*" Martina whispered.

"*Y tú,*" Jennifer returned.

Jennifer hurried over to Gage's side and they followed the path around to the church, where the jeep was parked. The driver, an older man in his late fifties, was just finishing tying down the back of a tarp.

Packages of all shapes and sizes had been set beside the church. A few people were carrying more inside.

"Supplies."

Jennifer glanced at Gage and realized he was studying the same thing she was. "Yes. But I wonder how long they last with the *federales* and *rebeldes* coming around?"

Gage's lips tight, he nodded. "Not long. And for all the community had, I noticed it was missing a lot of necessities."

"The war." Jennifer thought that summed it up.

"It's going to tear them apart before it's over with."

Hearing the bitterness in his voice, she remembered he had been assigned to a place that had witnessed this same thing. "Perhaps not with all of them, Gage," she said softly. "José is a man of prayer. I would say many of the people here are, too. Perhaps, together, with their prayers, things will turn out okay."

Gage only shook his head before moving past her to the driver. It was obvious in only seconds that the driver spoke no English.

Jennifer smiled. "Trying to convince him to go to Paulo?" she asked sweetly.

Gage scowled. "We're *not* going to Lahara, no matter what you want. I'm telling you, Jennifer, it's dangerous."

"Any more dangerous than where we are now?"

Gage opened his mouth then snapped it shut. "Would you tell him I want to go to Paulo and would gladly compensate him?"

Jennifer debated then shrugged. Smiling, she fired off what turned into a five-minute rapid Spanish discussion.

Finally, she turned back to him.

"Well?"

She shrugged again. "We're going to Lahara. He can take us to Paulo tomorrow if you're still interested, but there are troops that way right now and the only safe road is the one to the mission."

He narrowed his eyes, then sighed. "Fine. Anything is better than being on foot. Let's go."

He clambered into the back of the truck and waited. Jennifer slid in beside him, thanking the driver again. "You don't have to be upset," Jennifer soothed.

He didn't comment as the vehicle came to life with a loud cough then roar. Jennifer and Gage waved goodbye to the children and others who stood there watching them leave.

"I don't like missions," he finally admitted.

Jennifer was surprised that he actually acknowledged it. It had been obvious to her for sometime. "Why, Gage?"

Gage shrugged.

Jennifer bounced, banging her hip against the side of the jeep. She grabbed it and hung on, waiting for him to reply.

At her continued silence, he relented. "They believe too much."

Believe too much. She wondered what he meant.

But as she studied him, seeing the white-knuckled grip he had on the door and the tick in his jaw she realized there was something more. "What happened at a mission, Gage, that you believe that way?"

A sneaking suspicion entered her mind and she waited.

Gage's mouth tightened. He shook his head.

Jennifer wouldn't take no for an answer this

time. She had a feeling this was at the root of his problem. It all made sense to her now.

She realized she loved him. Her heart hurt too much as she watched him struggle for her feelings to be anything else.

"Please, Gage." She reached out to touch him again.

He spoke before she could entreat him further. "I went to one, in Korea, once I found out my mom was sick. They couldn't help me. My prayers didn't help. There was nothing I could do—I couldn't even be there. My sins had kept my prayers from reaching God."

Aching, she reached out. "Oh, Gage," she whispered. No wonder he feared betrayal by God, was afraid to go to God personally.

Just then they hit another huge bump, throwing them up, then down.

Jennifer cried out in pain as she was slammed up against the side of the jeep and thrown forward.

Strong arms encircled her just before she would have crashed to the floor.

Jennifer gratefully leaned into him, rubbing her hip while Gage soothed her aching shoulder.

When the pain eased, Jennifer expected Gage to let her loose. Instead, he continued to hold her. She felt totally secure and allowed her head to fall against his chest. "You know, Gage, one day you're going to have to trust again. One day you're going to have to believe not everyone is out to betray you."

"Let it drop, Jenny."

"I can't, Gage. You're going to have to trust someone. You don't want to love because you fear pain and betrayal. I know that. But pushing God away isn't the answer. Pushing me away isn't going to work, either."

Jennifer lifted her head, allowing her love to shine in her eyes. "You're going to have to trust me sooner or later."

Gage shrugged, his eyes going blank. "You won't be there forever. Sooner or later you'd leave, too."

Jennifer slid her hand up to his cheek. "I'd protect you from that pain if I could. I'd give my life if it were possible at this moment to make you understand that someone cares. But only God can convince you that you can trust again."

Gage held her close. In a whisper in the darkness he finally confessed, "I can't go to God. If I went to God and it failed I'm afraid I'd lose what little faith I have left."

Jennifer slipped her hands around Gage and held him tight, trying to pass some of her own encouragement to him.

Oh, please, Father, help me find a way to show Gage that he is worth something, that You care, that I care. I don't know what to do. I need Your guidance more than ever.

A choking and sputtering sounded and suddenly she and Gage were jerked forward as the truck's engine died.

Gage loosed his hold and she pulled back.

"What? What is it?"

Grimly, Gage said, "Can't you guess? The way our luck is going?" Glancing through the dark at her he continued, "The jeep has broken down and it looks like we are again stranded in the jungle miles from any inhabitants."

Chapter Fourteen

"**W**ell where else did you expect us to spend the night? There's no Hilton."

Gage growled low, under his breath. The woman was going to drive him batty. Two hours. It'd only been light two hours and she had twisted every word he said. "I didn't say I expected to spend the night in the Hilton, *chérie,* only that it would have been nice to have slept somewhere other than the back seat of a jeep."

"It beats the jungle floor," she muttered.

"So, how far are we now from that town you want to go to?" Jennifer continued to dodge leaves, smacking at them as she went, muttering under her breath the entire time.

The guide had gone off in the other direction back toward the village. Gage had refused to follow. He was tired of this and wanted to go home, not back to the village where they might have to wait another day or two until the guide could get some help to get him back to the mission. "About five minutes since the last time you asked, *chérie*."

"I want out of this jungle," he heard Jennifer mutter behind him. "I am never going near a jungle again. When I get home I promise I'm going to take five baths a day."

Gage turned to look at her and grinned. "It was ten baths a few minutes ago."

She shot him an exasperated look and continued on walking.

Gage shook his head. "I tell you, *chérie,* you can't make up your mind. You want to get those kids, you love the heat, then you want to go home and can't get out of here fast enough. Your mind works like rotelli noodles...going in so many different directions I can't keep up with you."

"Like you really want to keep up with my thoughts, Gage Dalton."

Gage laughed. The woman was always good

for a chuckle. "Well, I'll tell you. I'll be glad to get back to the city and turn you over to someone. Then my job will be done. I won't have to worry anymore."

Gage continued onward, studying the path ahead, thinking how he felt a bit empty at that thought. He wouldn't let Jenny know that, though. He stepped up his speed, a bit agitated. "The other pilot will be able to come down here and pick you up. You can do whatever you want, go after those kids, go chase villagers for all I care, even go categorize a few more birds."

She didn't answer and he shrugged, following the curving path around a large overhang of vines. He didn't like Jenny's silence, but refused to face her sad-eyed look. Of course, Jenny probably never had a sad-eyed look. It was only his guilty conscience for prodding her that made him think she'd look that way. Her eyes were probably shooting sparks. "I'll be done with this trip. I'll be back home to find out who those guns belong to and I won't have to worry."

When she still didn't comment, he broke down and asked her, just to hear her voice, "What do you think of that?"

Gage waited for her snappy reply. When she

didn't comment he decided she was going to be stubborn and not answer him.

Last night he'd confessed too many things. He'd been angry and furious over that. He wasn't comfortable having her know so much about him...no matter how much he'd come to care for her.

Still, it rankled that she suddenly quietened and didn't say a word. "Well, Jenny? Cat got your tongue?" he asked, pausing to take a deep breath.

When she again didn't reply he turned around to prod her again. He opened his mouth but the question died there.

Jennifer Rose was nowhere to be seen.

His heart fell to his toes as he thought of all the dangers that could befall a person in the jungle.

Heart racing, he sprinted back along the path. He stopped short when he rounded the corner and found Jenny, standing there, a snake winding its way about her neck and arms.

Pale as a ghost, covered with a fine sheen of sweat she simply stared at him through glassy eyes not moving, barely breathing as the huge constrictor wound its way around her.

"Jenny!" Gage started forward. What made him hear the click, he wasn't sure. But he did and automatically recognized it as the sound of an M-16 being set to fire. He stopped dead and turned his head to the sound.

"Very wise, amigo," the dark Central American man said. "You move and she dies. Or maybe she dies anyway."

Gage heard the whimper and turned back to Jenny, only to see the snake winding up her body. Her breathing was rapid, shallow. If she didn't hyperventilate soon, her eyes told him she was going to lose it.

"What do you want?" Gage's eyes locked with Jennifer's, willing her to stay calm even though his own heart was in his throat.

Four men.

Two to the left, one to the right and one behind. There was no way he and Jennifer could escape. And as for what game the men were playing and why, he had no idea.

"You have something that belongs to us. We want it back."

The rebels, he thought. It had to be. These were not the *federales*. So at least now he had an idea who they were and that told him what they wanted.

"In the plane."

Suddenly, everything was as clear as the blue sky above. He'd give the rebels anything to keep Jennifer from being hurt. And like a ton of bricks falling on his head, he suddenly knew why.

He loved her.

Despite his anger, his denial, his urge to protect his heart, he'd fallen in love with the spunky, sassy woman.

"We've already searched. It's not there."

It suddenly dawned on Gage these men spoke very good English. Curious, he wanted to turn and reexamine the rebels, but he dared not take his eyes from Jenny. She was more important. Not letting her lose her cool and risk getting shot was of utmost importance. Still, he had to try to negotiate with these men, too. He had to keep them talking so they didn't get angry. He wondered if they'd believe him if he told the truth. "If it's not in the plane, then I don't know where it is."

"Then the woman dies."

Jenny whimpered again either at the man's

words or because the snake began to coil itself around the middle of her body. Or maybe both.

''You didn't even tell me what you're looking for!'' Gage cried out, frustrated, knowing he'd risk getting shot before he stood there and allowed Jenny to be crushed in front of his eyes.

He tried to impress upon her with his eyes not to panic, to let her know what he was feeling, to lend her strength while he racked his brain for a way out of this.

Because he was so intent, it took a moment for the rebel's next words to register.

''So, the woman tells the truth. She said you knew nothing about what she was doing. That it was only her.''

Gage blinked, thinking he had misunderstood. Slowly, his gaze left Jenny's pleading one to focus on the short man on his left. ''What did you say?''

''She said she was the double-crosser, the one who delivered the guns but kept back the rest we were owed. I didn't believe her.''

Dizziness assailed Gage. Unreality crept up on him as he digested the words. *Double-crosser.* A roaring filled his ears.

He saw the man shrug. Then, with an evil smile, he said, "I guess I was wrong."

Gage watched as he suddenly pointed his gun and fired.

Despite the feeling of unreality, Gage cried out, horrified as he watched for Jenny to fall. Instead, the snake jerked then dropped lifelessly in a loose heap around her body.

Gage stared at it, wondering if they had really planned to let the snake hurt Jenny at all. Or had it all been a way of paying back a compatriot who had tried to cheat them?

Jennifer didn't move or say anything, just stared at him in mute horror.

He'd known.

Deep down he'd known she'd eventually betray him.

"You used me." He whispered the words, unable to utter anything more.

Obviously, neither could Jennifer. She laughed a funny little, half-hysterical laugh, then her eyes suddenly rolled back in her head and she fell forward.

Gage barely had a chance to catch her before she hit the ground.

He wanted to let her fall.

And then again he didn't.

The decision was taken out of his hands when the man in charge waved his gun. "Pick her up. We're going to have a talk when she wakes up. And if she doesn't tell us where our missing money is, you're both as good as dead."

Chapter Fifteen

The deep musty odor of dirt made Jenny's nose twitch. Motion rocked her body, making her aware of cold hard metal beneath the left side of her body.

It took a moment for it to register that she was in a vehicle similar to a jeep. And the vehicle was moving, rocking her back and forth.

Her head banged against the metal during a particularly rough bump and she winced. Blearily she opened her eyes.

Darkness met her gaze. Then she realized there was a darker shape just in front of her.

Her eyes adjusted to the darkness, to find a shadowed, but familiar face staring stonily down at her. Both arms were drawn behind him indicating he was bound.

"Gage."

Jenny realized she wasn't tied and pushed herself up to a sitting position beside Gage. Every bone in her body ached. "How long have we been here?"

"Several hours."

"Where are we?"

"Heading toward some town to be...questioned. But you'd know better than me."

His voice sounded different. Jenny cocked her head, trying to think why. Memories returned.

Shudders racked her body as she remembered the snake. Pain gripped her when she thought about the look on Gage's face.

Oh, how she'd hurt him. She wanted to cry when she remembered the disillusionment.

"I'm sorry."

Silence met her statement. Jennifer wondered if he'd heard her. She wanted to take him in her arms, soothe away the hurt she'd caused. Would he accept it? Jenny knew the one thing he couldn't handle was betrayal.

But she'd been trying to protect him. She

hadn't wanted the rebels to go after Gage, had hoped they'd leave him be if she lied....

"For what?" Anger vibrated in his voice.

"I lied, Gage. I'm not working for the rebels. I'm sorry you got hurt."

Gage laughed harshly, shocking Jennifer. "Try again, *chérie*. I know how you feel about snakes. You wouldn't have stood there and lied with a snake around you."

"I would if I loved you," Jennifer cried.

"Well, we both know that's not a problem now, don't we?" he drawled.

Jennifer sucked in a breath, hurt by his words. "I'm sorry, Gage. I know lying is wrong. Maybe I shouldn't have done it. Okay, I shouldn't have done it. I wasn't trusting God to handle the situation."

"You? Not trusting God?" He laughed harshly.

"I was wrong this time."

Gage shrugged and it infuriated her. "One day you're gonna realize people care about you. You're going to realize God cares, too, and you're going to go to God and ask Him to forgive you for your stubborn insistence that no one can really care. You're going to confess your fear of letting anyone care. And maybe, just maybe, you'll find it in your heart to forgive me, too, for hurting you.''

"Oh, I doubt that, *chérie*. I doubt I'll ever forgive you for what you've done.''

A crushing sense of defeat swamped her. "There's nothing I can do to convince you I wasn't in on this?''

"Why don't you tell me, *chérie,* how the rebels got hold of you.''

Jennifer wondered if he really wanted to hear her explanation. She didn't care. He'd asked. She was going to take the opportunity to tell him.

"I almost tripped over a shoestring. I paused to tie it. You were going on and on about getting back to town so I wasn't in the best of moods.''

Jennifer shifted closer, trying to find a comfortable position in which to sit as they bounced back and forth over the rutted road. She tried to ignore the two men in the front of the jeep as they talked and block out their sharp barks of laughter that punctuated their discussion.

"I dawdled on purpose, thinking it'd serve you right if you walked on down the path without me. Once you were out of sight I followed again, not wanting you too far away since the jungle can be sort of dangerous.''

Jennifer shuddered. ''The snake had crawled out into the path from the time you passed to the time I came upon the spot. I jumped, barely keeping from screaming—''

''I don't see how after last time,'' Gage interrupted sarcastically.

''I was afraid to draw unwanted attention. But it was too late. Those rebels were following us, closing in. I jumped and backpedaled, trying to get away. I obviously showed my terror because when I backed into one of the men who had decided to make himself known, it didn't take him long to figure out the snake bothered me.

''It also didn't take long for him to drape it over me.''

''Why didn't you run?''

Jennifer clasped her hands together. ''It's pretty hard to run when the leader is holding a pistol to your head, demanding you turn over his money or he's going to shoot.''

The horror of the situation made Jennifer's hands turn to ice. ''It was the gun or the snake.''

''Why didn't you just give them the money? Or did you leave it back in the States?''

Jennifer gaped, realizing he still didn't believe her. "Gage, I didn't know what they were talking about. And once the snake was on me, I was too terrified to move."

"Afraid your friends were going to kill you?"

Jennifer shook her head sadly. "No. I was afraid the rebels were going to find you and shoot you. I—I—I thought maybe they'd just let you go if I said I was the one who'd taken the money and that you didn't know anything about it."

"Stop it."

Jennifer jumped at Gage's harsh words. "What?"

"Stop lying. I've heard enough."

"But, Gage—"

"No. Let me tell you, *chérie*. You had me believing you. I honestly believed that those guns got into the plane some other way. You look too innocent, too sweet...

"But you got caught and now they want their money." He dropped his head, his shoulders drooping wearily. "You almost had me convinced."

Heart aching, Jennifer turned back to lean against the side of the jeep. *Father in heaven, what am I going to do? I was wrong to lie. I thought one small lie to protect him—but it backfired. I love him so much.*

But he hates me.

It's my own fault. I shouldn't have lied. I should have realized the rebels wouldn't let him go no matter what I said. I should have trusted you.

Jennifer felt tears well up in her eyes. *He's just hurting. If he really didn't care, he would have deserted me in the jungle. He wouldn't be hurting so much now over my supposed betrayal.*

Jennifer let her tears fall. *I've never trusted him. I've followed him, but not trusted him, not trusted You to work everything out.*

Bitterly, she thought about her own actions. *Though I have preached trust and forgiveness the entire time, Father, it's only now I realize that for all of my grand words, I never trusted Gage or You. If I had, I wouldn't have doubted the fact that You had a reason why Gage and I were stranded together. I wouldn't have done so many things I did.*

Trust.

And now it was too late to trust that Gage had

known what he was doing and would get her safely to a city.

What a fool I've been, Father. How can I convince him I trust him? What can I do? How can I show him I really love him.

Jennifer avoided sniffing, not wanting Gage to hear her pain made audible. *Please God, forgive me for my lack of trust. Please intervene, work out this problem as I trust You to handle all things.*

Jennifer felt a peace flood her as the Holy Spirit comforted her and reassured her. She dropped her head back, marveling at God's love and His patience with her. *Thank you, Father, for Your love,* she whispered silently.

A sudden exclamation from the front of the jeep sounded just before her entire world went crazy.

A squealing herd of wild pigs raced out into the road—spooked from something in the jungle. The driver jerked on the wheel to avoid them. The vehicle tilted and then rolled.

Jennifer screamed.

Gage shouted.

She grabbed him then was torn loose as she

was thrown first one way and then another in the back of the jeep.

The jeep turned on its side and slammed into a tree. Then all was quiet.

"Jennifer...Jenny? *Chérie?*"

Vaguely she heard the words.

Her head tingled where it had hit the side of the vehicle. Blinking she looked around.

Gage was bending over her. His face was twisted in a grimace.

"Are you hurt?" Was that her voice that sounded so weak?

"Banged up my leg. Come on, we've got to get out of here before that other jeep up ahead comes back."

"But we're prisoners," she argued, then realized she was making no sense. She touched her head trying to sort out her thoughts.

Gage shook his head. Jennifer saw his features soften and registered his concern.

"*Chérie*, we have to go."

Jennifer heard the determination in his voice. She pushed herself up to obey and moaned in pain. Her head felt as if someone had struck it with a hammer.

She swayed, grabbing at the side of the jeep,

which was actually the roof. Her hands clawed down the side until she fell against it.

"Chérie?"

She heard worry in Gage's voice. "I'm fine. Just a bit dizzy."

She worked her hands back up the side of the jeep and slowly pushed herself away. Gage had already climbed out and limped toward the front. Jennifer followed much more slowly. Reaching up, she touched her tender head and came away with bloody fingers.

Dumbly she stared at her hand.

"Get his knife."

Jennifer looked up at Gage's sharp command. She stumbled forward and looked at the man lying there, at her feet.

Jennifer realized he was dead. Black dots appeared before her eyes and she trembled...her knees giving slowly out as she wilted down to the ground.

"Chérie, honey, I am sorry. We don't have time for this."

She felt an arm touch her shoulder, realized Gage had knelt down by her, but didn't answer, couldn't answer. All she could think about was this was another soul with no chance now to change his ways.

"Jenny?"

Jennifer took a deep breath, reached to the man's belt and pulled out the knife. A moan from the jeep distracted her and she saw that the driver was gaining consciousness.

The sound of the other vehicle growing louder told her it was coming back so the others could find out what had happened to this one.

"Cut the ties on my hands."

Jennifer looked up at Gage.

He looked softly down at her. "You can do it, Jenny."

"Of course I can," she said, though with no conviction.

"It's shock," he told her reassuringly.

"I'm fine," she argued.

He turned and held his hands out. She looked at the knife then at the ropes on his hands. Finally, she slipped the knife over the bonds. They parted instantly.

Gage whirled around, tossing the ropes down. He snatched the knife in one hand and Jenny's arm in the other. "Come on."

He helped her up and took off in a flash, urg-

ing her along with him. Jennifer's headache
screamed at the abuse of running through the
jungle. The dots in front of her eyes came and
went. Her stomach turned with nausea.

The only thing that saved her was Gage's in-
jury. His leg hurt him so he kept having to slow.
Almost immediately though, he would again be
dragging her.

When they heard distant shouts, Gage doubled
his speed. ''They're going to be looking for us
now. Fortunately, I don't think we're more than
a mile or two from the city of Paulo. We crossed
the river just before you came to.''

''Only a mile?'' Jennifer tried to register that.
''Then we're safe?''

''Not yet. We need to get checked into a hotel
there and I need to make a call to find where the
American representative would be. Then we'll
be safe.''

Jennifer nodded. There would be a representative in the capital. Though it was small, America had been dealing with San Gabriel, trying to
gain permission for different studies and har-
vesting of plants in their forests, as well as wanting some of its exports.

Of course, with the political climate, the

American government might have already pulled out their representatives. That was why she'd been in such a hurry to get the kids, because of the way the government was. Of course, if she had trusted God, she would have accepted that He'd make a way when there had seemed no way.

She shook her head, deciding not to go down that path again. She would simply follow Gage and trust God to get them both to the city safely, no matter what he believed or not.

Chapter Sixteen

In minutes they were on the outskirts of the city. Gage kept hold of her arm, deftly leading her up and down streets that all blurred together for her. He knew where he was going, at least.

Jennifer only wanted to lean against him and rest. But that wasn't to be. Before she knew it, Gage headed into a hotel.

It was a one-story structure, stretching back several units. Large trees were planted every few feet.

He picked up the phone, and in halting Spanish, asked for the airport. He then handed the phone to the person at the front desk. What stumped her more was when he requested a room in Spanish.

Seeing her look he said, "I told you I know some basic Spanish. The people on the other end will make sure the bill is taken care of."

He started to turn back, then paused to look at her. She wasn't sure what he saw, but suddenly he slipped an arm around her.

The hotel manager handed them a key and rattled off the room number, still talking on the phone.

Gage took the key and steered Jennifer down the long walk to their room.

Inside, he closed the door before escorting her over to a chair. He tossed his backpack on the desk even as she pulled her own off and dropped it to the floor. "You stay right there and don't move. I've gotta take care of my leg."

Jennifer, feeling the stuffed-cushion chair give under her aching body, could only nod.

He paused at the bathroom door. "I mean it, *chérie*. If you run out on me, I'll find you."

Jennifer wanted to cry, but she was just too tired. Surely he couldn't still believe she was guilty.

She stared at the bathroom door in despair.

Trust in me and lean not onto your own understanding.

Trust. Trust. Trust. She would trust God in this. She loved Gage. But she could not force Gage to love her.

She heard muttering, noises and then the bathroom door opened. "Are you okay?" she asked.

He glanced at her as he came out of the bathroom. "I probably tore a few tendons, but other than that, yes, I'm okay."

Gage limped over to the phone and haltingly put in a call to the United States and Baton Rouge. "Sam, it's me."

Gage sank wearily against the desk. "Yes, yes. I'm fine."

He paused. "Yes, Ms. Rose is fine, too."

Slowly a sardonic eyebrow went up. "Is that so? Well, no. There's no coup that we see, but I'm sure she'll be glad to know her church held an all-night prayer meeting for our safety."

Jennifer wished Jake was there right now so she could hug him. Tears pricked her eyes again as she said a silent thank-you to God for leading her to such a good church.

"No. The plane has had it. There were guns...you heard?"

There was a longer pause. "So, Miguel is down here straightening everything out. I called the airport, asked a friend there to cover this room. Can you wire him the money?"

Gage rubbed a hand down his face. "Yeah. Okay. Thanks. Yes, she's fine. Send word to her pastor."

Gage listened a minute then hung up.

Neither said anything into the ensuing silence. Gage stood with his head drooped forward on his chest as he thought.

Jennifer just sat. She hurt. Her head was still pounding. "I think I'm going to shower," she finally said, deciding that would help her more than anything.

She stood.

Gage's gaze snapped up to hers. Weariness etched his features. "The business is under investigation."

"Oh, Gage," Jennifer said in sympathy. "But your pilot, Miguel, is down here working on it, right?"

Gage shrugged. "And Sam's working on it from the other end. Who knows what's going to happen. When word gets out, our business is likely to be destroyed by rumors."

Jennifer crossed to Gage, touching his arm. "Trust God, Gage. He can turn this whole mess around—"

Gage shook his head. "It's too late."

Jennifer gripped his arm. "Why won't you trust someone? Why can't you just let someone care?"

Gage's eyes took on a banked panic. "Like who? I should trust you, Jenny? You, who lied to me, too?"

Jennifer let go of his arm and stepped back. "Yes, I lied. I lied to those rebels. I was wrong. I think your problem, Gage, is that if you stop being angry, you're really going to have to grieve. You've never grieved for anyone you lost, have you? For the pain they caused you? Instead, you've held on to that betrayal, using the excuse never to trust again to protect yourself from hurt and fear."

Gage snorted. "What do you mean?"

"You're scared to death to trust God. If you find someone who really cares, who can really love you, then you're going to have to realize you've been mad at God simply to keep from trusting others. Quite daunting, isn't it?"

"I'm not mad at God. I go to church, *chérie*.

I realize the only way to heaven is with a personal commitment to Him. I just don't believe it goes further than that.''

He was lying. She could see it in his eyes.

Jennifer shook her head, finally seeing a hole in his armor. Instead, she staggered from the pain that erupted in her head at the motion.

Gage reached for her but she stepped back. "You're wrong, Gage," she whispered, forcing words out through the pounding. "You know that if you go to God, He's going to envelop you in His love. He's going to insist you let go of your pain and move on, which would mean trusting again. It's just easier to blame God because the mission wouldn't help you, to blame me because of what that lying rebel might say, instead of facing your feelings.''

Gage's face twisted in anguish. "I'm not discussing this with you. I see no reason whatsoever to discuss this. We're going to see the American representative. You're going to tell him about those guns and that I didn't put them on that plane.''

Jennifer sighed. It was useless to try to change him. She turned toward the door.

"Jenny!"

Gentle hands grabbed her, one arm circling her waist. "What did you do to your head?"

Jennifer blinked over her shoulder at Gage, then winced when he touched the sore lump. "Ouch."

His hand came away bloody. "Your hair is streaked with blood. I knew you'd hit it, possibly had a mild concussion. But why didn't you tell me you were bleeding?"

"I forgot."

He looked like a man tormented, torn between which direction to take at a crossroads.

Believe in me, she said with her eyes.

He waffled, holding her, then finally released her. *I can't,* his gaze replied.

He reached down and jerked up her backpack, pulling it open. "You brought rags. Where are they? Let me get you one for your head....oh, Jenny..."

Bleak despair filled his eyes as he reached the bottom of the bag. He came out with a handful of bills...all one hundreds.

Jenny's eyes widened in dismay. *The money.*

At least they knew now where the money had disappeared to.

She began to laugh. "I don't suppose you'd

believe I didn't know it was there? Of course not," she continued, not letting him answer. "I just can't believe this. It's too funny. I should have just let you do the packing on the plane then none of this would have happened."

Black dots appeared in her eyes again and she realized she was about to pass out. She forced the laugh away, took two deep breaths, then looked up at Gage. "I know it's too late for anything between us. But I love you, Gage. I really do. I don't know how or why it happened, but there, it's said. Maybe it's because I know, deep down, you have a soft heart. I don't know. All I know is...I will always love you."

"Don't..." His voice was tortured, raspy. "Don't, Jenny. Please. I—I can't hear you say that."

Tears tumbled down her face, stamina and hope finally succumbing to her exhaustion. "Come on, Gage. It doesn't matter anymore. I give up."

"Jenny, *chérie*—" he started, only to be interrupted by the opening of the door.

A small dark-haired man slipped into the room, closing the door behind him. He was dressed in jeans and a leather jacket. His hair was neatly cut and he was passably handsome.

"Miguel."

The man who was supposed to have been her pilot, Jennifer thought.

"I'm glad you're here. How'd you find us?" Gage asked. He rubbed at the back of his neck. "Never mind. Right now we need a ride to the American embassy."

Gage didn't notice because he was still rubbing his neck. But Jennifer had no problem seeing Miguel pull out a gun. Her eyes widened in shock and she glanced over to where Gage stood, three feet to her left.

Gage chose that moment to look up. Shock and confusion registered before his eyes narrowed. "You were responsible for those guns!"

Miguel shrugged. "Everything would have been fine if you'd waited and let me fly the plane like I was supposed to."

Gage looked over at Jenny. She saw regret in his eyes.

"I need the money," Miguel continued. "You have made the people down here angry at the people I do business with back in the States.

I have to get them that money before my con-
nections in the States start hunting me, instead.''

Miguel stopped, his eyes suddenly riveted to
the bag on the desk near Gage. ''Ah, I see you
have my money. Good.''

''I don't suppose you're going to just leave
with it?'' Gage asked quietly.

Miguel shook his head. ''I'm afraid I can't do
that. Of course, with the way things are down
here right now, it will be perfectly understand-
able if you are both found murdered. No one will
raise much of a fuss.''

Gage's jaw tightened. ''I've talked to Sam,
Miguel. Someone is going to put it all together.
He said investigators were on their way down
here.''

Miguel shrugged. ''Then I'll have to relocate
again.''

Again. Jennifer got a sick feeling in her gut.
This man was a cold-blooded killer, who had
been practicing gunrunning for quite a while.
And his gun was aimed at Gage.

Just then she saw Gage's hand move.

The knife. Oh, no, he still had his knife. She
didn't even want to think about what he might
do, was going to do with it. She knew it had to

be done, whatever he did, so she'd try to help in any way she could. *Father, guide him. Your will,* she whispered.

"So, you're just going to kill us and leave?" Jennifer asked, trying to draw his attention.

Gage's eyes cut to her in surprise, then understanding.

"Unfortunately, yes, Ms. Rose. It's such a shame, too. I hate innocent parties being caught in the middle."

"Then let us go!" she cried, when he started to look back at Gage.

He turned his gaze back and Gage chose that moment to pull his knife and throw it.

Miguel grunted, staggering back against the wall, his curses filling the air as he slid down it.

Gage started forward but the gun came back up. Instead of losing the gun, Miguel still held it and was still conscious.

Hatred burning in his eyes, Miguel growled, "You're gonna die."

Gage's eyes widened in shock then resignation.

Miguel pulled on the trigger.

"Noooo!" Jennifer cried and launched herself at Gage.

A loud report sounded.

Jennifer felt as if she'd been hit in the back with a two-by-four. Her body slammed into Gage's.

"Jenny!" She heard Gage's cry, felt herself slide to the floor and tried to assimilate what had happened.

Noises could be heard, grunts and groans then Gage was there, over her. His hands hesitated and then he lifted her up against him.

An involuntary groan escaped Jennifer as a burning pain engulfed her back.

"I'm sorry, *chérie,* so sorry."

"I'm okay, Gage," she whispered, confused. "I'm just tired."

Jennifer watched, dumbfounded as tears welled and spilled over in Gage's eyes. "You were shot, Jenny."

She blinked, trying to make sense out of his words. "Oh," was all she could think to say.

Suddenly, the room was filled with people. They grabbed hold of the now unconscious Miguel. Someone yelled that the police had been called.

Gage barely registered what was going on around him. He looked down at the woman in his arms. The woman he loved, but hadn't trusted. "Please, Jenny. Forgive me. You were right. Don't leave me."

"What beautiful words," she murmured, slurring them a bit as her mind filled with a gray mist.

"Jenny, *chérie.* No. I have to tell you...Jenny?"

Gage stared down in fear at the still woman in his arms. "Don't die on me. Not now, Jenny. I have to tell you I love you."

"Excuse me, *señor,* but we need to take her to the hospital now."

Dazedly, Gage glanced up to see two men waiting to load Jenny onto a stretcher. He shook his head, surprised that an ambulance had already arrived.

Fresh tears ran down his face as he realized he just might be losing the woman he loved. And all because of his stubbornness. She had been right. He'd been so hurt that he'd used anger to keep everyone at a distance—even God. To forgive meant to risk again.

But Jenny had learned how to risk, to love after she'd lost everyone and everything. Why hadn't he been able to learn that from her?

In one bright flash of insight he realized he had. He *did* love again and had learned, during their trek through the jungle, just how to open up and care, though he'd never admitted it.

She had taught him, after all.

The sweet young innocent rose who had been crushed so many times had persevered to teach him about life and love.

And he suddenly knew a way he could repay her, show her that he had changed—if she lived.

He followed the stretcher to the ambulance, which was really just a converted army truck. Climbing in, he prayed, *Forgive me, Father, for my idiocy. I've been so blind. Thank You for sending this woman to open my eyes, to teach me about Your love again. Now, Father, please, intervene, save her. I know I was wrong. You do take a personal interest in our lives.*

Gage touched Jenny's head. "But if you choose not to save her, Father, I'll not turn my back on You again."

He lowered his head and kissed her forehead. "I'll never stop loving her, though."

And he'd never stop grieving, he thought, bleakly. Never.

Chapter Seventeen

The sound of the door whooshing open captured Jennifer's attention. Carefully, she pushed herself up in the bed and glanced hopefully at the door, only to be disappointed again.

"Well, if that's the face I'm gonna get every time I visit you, I might just stop coming."

Belatedly, Jennifer smiled. "Come on in, Jake."

Jake sidled in, a large canvas tote bag over one shoulder. He moved two of the bouquets of flowers from her small table and laid the tote bag on it. "Cards from all the kids at the day care."

"How sweet." She stared at the flowers Jake had moved.

Jennifer loved flowers. She had nearly two dozen arrangements in her Louisiana hospital room. The huge carnation display from Rand and Max all the way down to the small cluster of daisies and the three potted plants that people had graciously offered graced every spare inch in her room.

But the one thing she wanted most was missing.

She hadn't heard from him since that day in the hotel room. It had been two weeks.

Jennifer glanced back up to the news channel, the remote still in her hand.

She was startled when Jake reached over and took it from her, snapping the TV off.

"Jake!"

He smiled a gentle smile. "Honey, watching the news isn't going to bring him back. You just have to trust God."

Jennifer blinked at his words, thinking how true that was. The sting in her eyes wouldn't go away, though, as she thought about Gage, still down in San Gabriel. "It's been weeks. The government's still in an uproar. And now they've closed the borders. No one is allowed in or out. What if Gage got hurt? And the kids…"

Jake took her hand and squeezed it. "You are not to worry about those children. I promise you, we'll find a way to get them to the Richardsons. God has a plan, though we may not understand it now. Trust Him, Jenny.''

Jennifer nodded. ''I do, Jake. I just…worry. I've finally gotten over the past and don't blame myself, or anyone else for the unfortunate incidents that happened with my mother's day care. But…I just can't help but worry for Gage.''

Jake squeezed her hand again. ''Gage loves you, Jennifer. Would he have made sure you got out if he didn't?''

''But why didn't he come with me?'' she cried. ''Something must have happened.''

Jake frowned. ''We nearly lost you. Your lung was collapsed. You were unconscious for five days. It's amazing the recovery you've made in only two weeks. Be thankful for that, Jennifer, and let God handle the rest.''

She nodded.

''By the way, I've managed to get word to a missionary in San Gabriel. He's going to check to see if he can find out anything for us.''

Gratitude flooded Jennifer's eyes. ''Thank you.''

''Excuse me.''

Jennifer and Jake both turned to see a nurse standing at the door. ''There's a call for you, Pastor. It's a Dr. Richardson. Can you take it?''

"I'll be right back," Jake said as he left the room.

Jennifer rolled back onto her side. "No hurry," she replied, thinking how devastated the Richardsons probably had to be over her failure. Still, they had assured her they weren't and that God would work everything out.

"Father, protect Gage," she whispered. "I love him. I don't want to lose him."

"I don't want to lose you either, *chérie.*"

Jennifer gasped and with difficulty rolled over onto her back to see Gage, rumpled and disheveled, standing just inside the doorway. "Gage?"

She was almost unable to believe he stood before her.

"I'm sorry, *chérie,* that it's taken me so long to get back."

"Where have you been?" she cried, trembling with relief.

He hesitated by the door and Jennifer wondered at it until she suddenly realized it was insecurity. She opened her arms wide.

Gage might have been slow on getting over things, but he was no fool. He strode across the room and gathered her tenderly against him. "Oh, *chérie,* you look so good. I was so scared I'd never see you again."

Jennifer began to cry.

Gage rocked her. "*Chérie,* oh, *chérie,* don't cry. I'm so sorry, *ma petite.*"

The strength of him, the feeling of security as he held her, only fueled her sudden anger. "You could have been killed," she cried and pushed him away. "Where did you go? Why didn't you come back sooner?" She leaned forward and grabbed his arms.

Gage's eyes widened. "You were worried about me?"

Jennifer released him and fell back against the bed, indignant. "Of course not. Why would I be worried about you?" She started sobbing again and lurched back up, grabbing him around the neck.

Gage, thrown off balance, almost fell on top of her. But he didn't mind. Instead, he grinned like an idiot. "I had something I had to do, *chérie.*"

When she opened her mouth, he placed a finger over it. "*Non,* let me finish. You were right. I was hiding from God. I didn't want to risk anymore. I wanted an easy path with guarantees. It took you to show me that there are no guarantees in life."

Her eyes widened and he smiled.

"In a good way, *chérie.* Only in a good way. You see, I love you. And hiding from the world didn't stop those feelings. Sometimes you just have to take a chance and trust God.''

"But you said you don't believe God takes a personal interest.''

He smiled. She was determined to have a complete surrender from him or nothing at all. Oh, how he loved her. "I was proven quite wrong at Lahara Missions. I saw miracles there, *chérie*. The miracle of salvation reminded me of just how personal an interest God takes in our lives. And you know, I've wondered over the past weeks if perhaps my mom continued to lie to me because she couldn't face having me at home watching as she died. I'm not excusing her lies, but I think perhaps she just couldn't have handled both my grief and my sister's as she lay there dying. I've had a chance to talk with my sister on the way here to assure her I was fine and that's something she hinted at. It's the first time we've really talked about it. But we plan to have a get-together of all the family real soon and I'll be able to talk to her then.''

"Oh.''

Gage saw her face fall and knew what she was thinking. He leaned down and kissed her, gently.

When he pulled back tears glistened in her eyes again. "When are you leaving, then?''

A small smile played about Gage's lips. "That depends on you, *chérie*."

"It does?"

"I promised my sister that she'd see me when you and I walked down the aisle together and not before."

Confusion filled her eyes only for a moment before joy replaced it. "You mean...?"

He kissed her again, then took her hand in his. Staring into her eyes, he said, "I love you, more than my own life. These past weeks gave me plenty of time to study my life, what it has been like and why. I've found I've only really known peace and joy since you've come into it and that's because you loved me enough to point me back in the right direction—toward God.

"I've also found, I'm very lonely without you and can't imagine a future without you by my side. Will you, Jenny, *chérie,* do me the honor of becoming my wife?"

Tears spilled over again. "I'm a watering pot," Jennifer muttered, wiping at her eyes.

Gage caught her hand and kissed her tears away. "I like you any way you'll come to me, *chérie.*"

Jennifer smiled up at him, but there was a sadness in her eyes. "I'll be glad to marry you, Gage Dalton. But I have to go back into San

Gabriel first. I will not leave those children down there.''

Gage looked uncomfortable. ''Jenny, *chérie,* there's something I should tell you....''

''Jennifer, guess what? Gage is back and he brought the kids back with him.... Oh—'' Jake stopped just inside the doorway. Raising a brow he looked from one to the other. ''I see you've already heard.''

Jenny looked back and forth between the two. ''I don't think I've heard everything. What about the kids?''

Jake raised an eyebrow and Gage flushed. ''Gage is a hero down in San Gabriel. He helped save the mission and was able to rescue the children.''

''What? How?'' Jennifer looked from Gage to Jake and back.

Gage shrugged. ''Let's just say, you're going to marry a very well-connected man. I have a few good friends in the army who were able to pull some strings—especially when they learned children were involved.''

''Oh, Gage!''

He shrugged. ''I couldn't leave them there. They mean too much to you.''

Jennifer's heart swelled and felt as if it were

going to burst. "Then the Richardsons have the children now?"

Gage nodded.

"You know, Gage, I don't think I'll ever be happier than I am now."

"Except in paradise," Jake added referring to heaven, coughing slightly to remind them of his presence.

Jennifer nodded, agreeing. Yes, heaven would be a better place.

Reaching up she pulled Gage into her embrace. "Let me rephrase that," she whispered. "I think this is the happiest I'll be this side of paradise."

She heard Gage's reply just before he lowered his mouth to her lips. "Me, too, *chérie*. Me, too."

* * * * *

*Be sure to look for
Cheryl Wolverton's next book,
THE BEST CHRISTMAS EVER,
available in December
from Love Inspired.*

Dear Reader,

Where do my ideas come from? With this story I thought how funny it would be to pair an eternal optimist with a definite pessimist. And I just love action. So, I decided it would be fun to drop them in a jungle where they would be forced to work out their differences.

As I started writing the story, I thought about my hero, Gage, and his struggles. Sometimes it's hard to deal with the pain and betrayal of a loved one or trusted friend and go on. It's easier to keep everyone at arms' length. But that's not what God wants us to do. Our Heavenly Father wants to hold us and comfort us and teach us that no matter how much we hurt, He loves us and takes a personal interest in us.

I hope you enjoy Gage and Jennifer as they trudge their way through the San Gabriel jungle. Please write and let me know what you think at P.O. Box 207, Slaughter, LA 70777.

Best,

Cheryl Wolverton

Not The Same Old Story!

 Exciting, glamorous romance stories that take readers around the world.

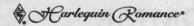 Sparkling, fresh and tender love stories that bring you pure romance.

 Bold and adventurous— Temptation is strong women, bad boys, great sex!

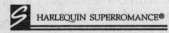 Provocative and realistic stories that celebrate life and love.

 Contemporary fairy tales—where anything is possible and where dreams come true.

 Heart-stopping, suspenseful adventures that combine the best of romance and mystery.

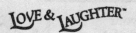 Humorous and romantic stories that capture the lighter side of love.

October 1998...

Love Inspired invites you to
experience the words of one of America's
best-loved writers...

Carole Gift Page

This talented author of over thirty-five
novels returns to Love Inspired with

RACHEL'S HOPE

Rachel Webber knew her unexpected pregnancy was a
blessing, but her joy was short-lived when her beloved
family began to unravel. Not only were she and her
husband, David, drifting further apart, but their
impressionable teenage son seemed to be suffering
most of all. Still, Rachel's enduring faith had always
illuminated her life. And now, more than ever, she had
to believe the good Lord would bring hope back into
all their lives....

Don't miss this emotional story about
the power of faith and love.

Available in October 1998 from

Available at your favorite retail outlet.

The author of over fifteen inspirational
romances, Irene Brand brings
Love Inspired® readers a poignant and
heartfelt story.

HEIRESS

by

Irene Brand

After discovering that she was the sole heiress to her
uncle's vast fortune, Allison Sayre embarked on an
amazing journey. She never imagined she would
uncover a shocking family secret. Or be drawn back
into the life of Benton Lockhart, a man whose
powerful spiritual convictions had once
inspired her....

Available at your favorite retail outlet from
Love Inspired.®

Steeple
Hill™

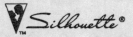

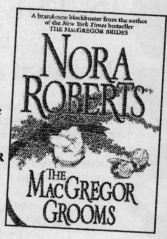

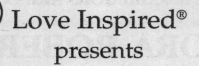

Love Inspired®

presents

A WEDDING IN THE FAMILY

by

Kathryn Alexander

Strong and tender Adam Dalton was
instantly intrigued by vulnerable single mom
Angela Sanders. He knew she had good reason to
be afraid of commitment, but he prayed that their
deepening feelings—and shared faith—would
ultimately lead to a wedding in the family.

Watch for
A WEDDING IN THE FAMILY
in October 1998

from

Available at your
favorite retail outlet.

ILIAWIF